HOME FREE

HOME FREE

James Calvin Schaap

CROSSWAY BOOKS • WESTCHESTER, ILLINOIS
A DIVISION OF GOOD NEWS PUBLISHERS

Cover illustration by Albert DeCandia.
Cover design by K. L. Mulder.

First printing, 1986.

Printed in the United States of America.

Library of Congress Catalog Card Number 85-70470

ISBN 0-89107-363-9

For Mary Hooper

ONE

The highways narrowed the closer they came to Easton—eight lanes through Chicago traffic, six through Milwaukee, a four-lane freeway north of the city, and finally a skinny county-trunk road humped with leveled scoops of blacktop where successive winter frosts had burst through the pavement like tiny volcanoes. They had been away seven years.

"So why are you so quiet?" Ila said, whispering herself.

Hank nodded toward the sleeping boy strapped into the safety seat in the back.

Ila brushed her hair and checked her face in the mirror clipped to the visor. "It's him, isn't it? Your father?"

He could feel her looking at him, but didn't want to answer her and have her pin him down that way. "Maybe," he said. "Yeah, maybe it is my father, but it's all of this out here, too." He pointed indiscriminately. "It's these woods. This road. It's me coming back here again. Every one of these farms has a face to me."

She slapped the visor up, drew a few long hairs from her brush and flicked them on the floor. "You can take the boy out of the country, I guess," she said, dropping the brush in her purse.

"It's all silly to a sophisticated city girl like yourself—"

"Not so loud, you'll wake him." Ila put a finger up to her lips.

"In ten minutes we'll be home anyway."

County Trunk A pushed west from the lakeshore, pencil-straight, cutting through broom grass meadows, long sloping bellies of plowed land, and black swampy patches of elm and birch—alongside, both ditches lined with fat cattails.

"Back in there," he said, "maybe a half mile or so, we used to look for arrowheads every spring. Once we even found one. The sand pushes up new stones in the spring, little pieces of flint, like chips. You ever see flint, Ila? It's kind of creamy smooth. Indians used it for arrowheads."

"Did your father take you out?" she said.

"Sometimes. Sometimes it was just a bunch of kids—you know, when we were ten or eleven." She kept looking at him, and he could feel her waiting, as if he were about to deliver a final judgment. "My father's not a bad man, Ila."

One thing—in ten years of marriage there was one thing that annoyed him about Ila, and that was the way she would suspend a conversation by hanging up his last words in emptiness. She'd speak, he'd speak, but then she'd turn silent, as if his last words were illustrations in themselves of his inherent silliness.

Finally she spoke. "Will you feel better if I tell you that I know he's okay?"

The trees had already shed their leaves in the fall winds, and against the gray overcast the trunks and branches seemed uniformly black, like an uneven pattern of bars against the open background.

"We won't even be here a week," he said. "And that's all. Sunday afternoon we'll leave for the tour. What is it?—four days? We'll pick up Tony a week later. Four days, that's it."

Half-twisted, with both her hands on the back of the seat, she kept her eyes on him. "Sometimes I'm sure that my husband, my husband the missionary, is crazy. One minute you're drowning in nostalgia—'there's where we used to find arrowheads'—and the next you're counting the hours before we leave." She turned completely and reached back to her son. "I wonder how your father will take to his grandson?"

"He'll spoil him rotten, just like any grandpa, maybe worse."

"You really think so?"

"I can't always take my father, but I understand him." He laid his hand on Ila's arm. "You wait. Dad will melt with Tony around. Buy him candy, take him to the park—I know how he'll act."

"Just don't let me catch you being jealous," she said. "Tony, Tony—honey? Wake up now. We're almost at your grandpa's house."

"See that barn there, Ila. Three summers in a row I put up hay in that barn. That one, right there. Terrible place to pack bales. No ventilation at all. Did I ever tell you about baling hay?" He heard the boy's breathing shift. "Must have been a wet fall; lots of corn out yet. See that place? Elmer Hudson's—he used to beat his kid. One day years ago some of the man's cattle died. Found out later it was his own kid that poisoned them. But I never told you that story, Ila. Actually, I hadn't thought of it until now."

"Maybe we should have got him up before. I know what's going to happen—he'll be as grouchy as ever when he meets his grandparents."

The boy whimpered. Ila pulled Tony over the back of the seat and into the front, set him on her lap, and whispered to him. The boy rubbed his round fists into his eyes, and Ila pulled his head down against her chest. "There, there," she said, "your Grandpa and Grandma are *so* anxious to see you. They never saw little Tony yet, only a picture."

"You wait till Dad gets ahold of him," Hank said.

The road rose slowly, climbing the hill just east of town.

"Look at those houses, Ila. That's all new out here. Ten years ago that was a pea field. We used to sit out there all afternoon and eat peas—till we got the runs."

"Even here things change, Hank," she said, as they drove into town.

But the streets looked the same to him, turn-of-the-century houses down both sides, big two and three story frames with peaks and gables and, inside, he knew, tall oak baseboards and high ceilings. Unheatable houses. The warm houses he grew up in. Main Street—a march of graying maples, monster trees, their top branches, leafless in November, flung up over the village, and here and there along the street, a stump or a gap where age itself had toppled one of them, turned decades of shaded summers into November warmth for a fireplace in somebody's den. He turned left where he always had turned left.

It was more than seven years really; it was closer to fifteen, aside from a weekend visit now and then at the end of a semester years ago. Hank Pietenpol went away to college when he graduated from high school, and he rarely returned home for any length of time, not even during his undergraduate years. He preferred working away from Easton, living on his own with some other kid looking forward to seminary, or spending his summers painting houses in the city where he attended college.

Then Ila arrived from Chicago, during his junior year. They were married when he graduated, and she worked on campus while he spent three more years in seminary. Christmas visits they would take with Hank's folks, and maybe a few days in August; and once every six months or so, Wim and Corrie, his folks, would drive around the lake to Michigan to see their son and his Chicago wife. Short and semi-sweet, their visits were then.

Hank and Ila left on a mission to El Salvador seven years ago; four years later Tony was born. After the seven years, a furlough; the church rented them a home in Chicago, and, back in the States for ten months, Hank planned to study.

"That's new—that gas light out front of the house. You remember that, Ila?" Close to the street stood an old-style glass lantern on a black pole, with a die-cast silhouetted hunter shouldering a shotgun, his dog, tail pointed sharply, in front of him. And beneath the hunter, in white letters—William J. Pietenpol.

Ila pulled her coat around herself and the boy.

He couldn't help thinking how hard it must have been for his father to dig a trench for the lamp—through his precious lawn.

His father and mother were standing at the doorway as if they had expected them this very second. Hank waved from the driveway. He decided they hadn't changed much; his mother looked heavier maybe, in the arms, and his father, if anything, lighter, shoulders stooped slightly. Ila carried Tony to the house.

When he opened the trunk, he heard his mother's voice pitch upward in her old uneasy laughter. He knew she was reaching for her only grandchild. He pulled out the two biggest suitcases.

"You have any trouble, Hank?" his father asked.

Hank felt his father's presence in the ends of his fingers, in his back, the back of his neck, as if Wim Pietenpol suddenly stood between himself and the sun.

"No," he said, "no trouble at all. Real smooth driving."

"You had maybe bad traffic in Chicago?"

Hank rifled through the trunk, as if he were busy rearranging. Diffuse emotions made him want to cry. Something between anger and pity he felt for the man's stubborn and awkward inability to say something more meaningful—after more than seven years—than a question about traffic in a city three hours away. "It wasn't a bother at all," he said. "Think you can help me out with these?"

"Ja, you let me take these big ones here. Too heavy maybe for the ministers of the gospel." It was like his father to say it that way, in a light tone, as if he meant it as a joke. His father slapped him slightly across the upper arm. "But what is it—my own son forgets even to shake his father's hand?"

"I'm sorry, Dad—all the unloading and everything—"

What was left of his hair was plastered down against his temples and trimmed up above his ears. Thinner maybe, Hank thought, maybe a little thinner through the shoulders. And it was the same old homecoming welcome pinch around his fingers, locking his hand. His own slight grip embarrassed him. His father was always quicker; he would always beat him to the grip. It was something he had to put up with, Wim Pietenpol always gunning for his own masculinity. Beating him to the grip would have been like talking back to his father.

With his other hand Wim squeezed his shoulder. "Ja," he said, "Corrie says it is so good to have you home, and Ila, and the boy."

Hank nodded and smiled, his father's hand pumping his like it always did. "It's good to be home again, Dad," he said.

"I suppose down there where you preach the men kiss each other on the cheeks."

"Sometimes they do," he said.

"On television it always looks so silly," Wim said.

Hank didn't want to quit shaking. He didn't want to relax his own weak grip because he didn't want to be the first to let go.

Inside, the old shiny hardwood floors were covered with throw rugs now, in different colors and different weaves. Undoubtedly each swatch had been purchased during a different sale, at times when the bank account allowed a purchase of that size. It seemed a shame to cover wood floors the way his parents did, but the rugs didn't surprise him. Wim and Corrie Pietenpol had both come over as children from the old country, Holland. To them hardwood floors were no romantic emblem of some golden age, so they buried them beneath rugs, reds and blues, greens flecked with silver, because a rug was something warm beneath your feet in January, something to cushion the chill from hardwood floors—the hardwood floors you scrubbed on calloused knees when you had no money for rugs.

His mother kissed him and hugged him lightly, one of her arms already full of her grandson.

"It's Grandma, Tony. Can you say 'Grandma?' "

The boy looked away as if he weren't involved in the conversation. He seemed almost at home in the arms of the strange, heavy woman.

"He likes you, Mom," Hank said. "There must be something in him—some gene or something—that recognizes you as his Grandma." He put the suitcases just off the rubber mat over the rug at the front door.

"He looks just like his pretty mother," Corrie said. "See his nose and mouth." She poked at him, at either cheek, trying to provoke a smile. "Do you have Mommy's smile too, Tony? Sure you do, sure. I think there's a smile there too, Grandpa. Ja, I see one coming right here." She tickled him at the corner of his lips. "Here—here—see it, Mom? It's his mother's smile too. You see it there, Grandpa?"

Tony turned his face away into his Grandma's shoulder.

Corrie had written them every week for the last seven years—"Sunday afternoon" the letter would say, at its top right hand corner. But every three months or so his father would sit down. "Here now, Wim," Hank could imagine his mother having said, "you sit once and write. They are your children after all, too." Wim was an awkward writer, but energetic, his lines sometimes laced with jokes, unusual for him since Hank never considered his father a jocular man. But every time he wrote, Wim would mention Corrie's health: "Corrie is good, too, and for this we thank God." His mother never said anything about her health; she would have considered it unworthy of their concern, Hank being a missionary, doing God's work so dutifully.

"So give me the son of yours once before he gets to be a Mama's boy," Wim said. He held out both arms, but Tony wouldn't leave his grandma. "Come to Grandpa," he said.

"Ach, Wim, sometime later you can have him. When they're little like Tony they belong to the women yet. Isn't that right, Ila?"

It surprised Hank to hear Ila agree.

The house had changed somewhat in seven years. Different pictures decorated the walls. His mother never could stand any open walls, it seemed. A wall without a picture made her think that someone was in the process of moving out. So her walls were hung with all manner of wisdom and inspiration—mostly Bible verses in windswept calligraphy, some wood-burned epigrams from Spurgeon, and here and there something unflinchingly romantic from Emerson or Coleridge. Having been gone for years, Hank recognized the inherent moralism of the place, as if the dining room alone were a museum of famous quotations, most of them from Proverbs.

And there was the dark brown tablecloth already spread over the dining room table, ready for Thanksgiving dinner, just like always.

"So what do you think, Hank—the old house look the same?" his father said.

"Mom's got more plaques than she ever had before—"

"I tell you that woman takes nothing down. 'If I take one off the wall,' she says to me, 'then I feel like maybe I don't believe anymore what it says.' So I tell her to put one up in the basement then, or on the stairs, or in a bedroom. 'Which one?' she says. 'How can anybody say which one of these isn't so good as the others anymore?' " His brows hunched up as if the whole business was beyond anyone's comprehension. "So the walls keep filling up. Pretty soon maybe everything will go—the whole business, just like the walls of Jericho—phfft—"

"—buried in Bible verses," Hank said.

"For Corrie that would be the best way to die." His

father walked out of the dining room. "I've got to hold that boy," he said. "His grandma will spoil him."

Wim Pietenpol told Corrie to turn on the lights when his son couldn't get the slide projector to reverse.

"It's in the way you bite on your words sometimes," he told Hank. "I can hear it, that Spanish sound. And sometimes you sing on the vowels—'to-GEH-ther'—like that." He fiddled with the projector knobs, tipping his glasses down on his nose.

Hank stood back and watched his father's thick, mechanic's fingers. "We speak English at home at times. You know, for Tony. But otherwise it's only Spanish. It's an adjustment to have to use English again. Seven years—"

"I could tell you once what it was like for your grandparents to come to this country with no English." Wim kept his head down over the projector. "And not so many here that could understand the Dutch language. For us it wasn't so bad—we were only kids."

"I know what it must have been—"

"There is nothing so bad as not knowing the language. So my father always told us. Not even poverty is so bad," he said, looking up; his eyes held some deeper memory. "They stopped us from speaking Dutch right away. 'You learn the English now,' Pa said."

"It's not easy. We had to get by with what we knew of Spanish—"

"Ach, one whole year of language training you and Ila had in California. Who was here to give to us some words to use in this country? You don't know, Hank. And besides, you had a job already, waiting for you, a job what people respected, too. You were big already before you got there." His back was bent over the machine, his fingers picking and pushing. Corrie sat in the big new chair with her finger up on the light switch.

Wim clicked the controls and the projector spun the carousel of slides forward. "I got to open this up, Hank," he said. "And who knows what I will find in there—this church machine. Nobody pays much attention to church machines. They just use them." He looked up at Hank over the rims of his glasses. "Friday night, you know—Friday night you will have to use this one yourself in church."

"Tomorrow open it up, Dad. We'll get by without reverse."

"It's the principle. You was never one to take to machines. But you know the Lord gives to us this kind of technology for our use and care, like all of creation." When he straightened his back, he put his hands on his sides, thumbs forward. "Go on, then. For seven years Corrie and I been waiting to see the slides." He took a step or two backward to the couch, put a hand on the arm rest and lowered himself next to his daughter-in-law. "Tomorrow I get to that machine." Tony climbed up on his grandfather's lap.

The wall made an adequate screen for the slides, Hank thought, except for the nail head up there that spotted every picture. Wim had taken the big landscape down from the front room wall, the one of a mountain cabin, a chalet, with a little nervous creek cutting across the foreground. It had never before struck him to try to guess what there was in the picture that fascinated his parents, lowlanders from the days of their births in the old country. Now it seemed odd that they would celebrate some Bavarian dream in their Midwestern living room. "That looks good," Corrie probably had said one day, shopping for an egg-beater in a discount store.

Hank flashed the first picture up on the wall. "This is where we live," he said. "But we sent you a picture of our house before, didn't we?" He spoke over his shoulder at his father.

"That house looks better yet up there when the picture is big," Wim said. "At first, years ago, when you said Central America, Corrie and me thought it would be those poor people with mules and the pots on the women's heads, you know. And in the jungle—eh, Corrie?"

"Here's the church, but you've seen that before too," Hank said. "You can see we're in a kind of suburban area—you have to go for miles before you'd get to any kind of jungle."

"Just not so fast now, Hank. We want to see this good here."

The church projector appeared new, the whirr of the fan barely audible.

"Is that a block church?"

"Stucco."

"No winters there?" Corrie said.

Ila said it was seven years since they had seen snow.

"But are you happy, Ila?" Corrie said. "That is what is really important. Tell me once—are you happy?"

Hank waited for his wife to answer.

"Maybe it's not always like being home, but we're getting used to it," she said. "I guess for Tony it will be home. You can look at it that way, I guess."

"Here's some people from church." The camera had caught smiles on people's faces, old and young, children in a variety of brown skin tones. "That man with the short hair in the front is an officer of the church. His name is Juan—"

"He's got ten children," Ila said.

"You got no problems with the race business there, Hank?" his father said. "They all get along together so nice like a rainbow."

Hank stopped on a slide of the backyard garden. "Race isn't such a big thing like it is in the States. But it's there—discrimination, prejudice—and you get to feel it after a while. The people are careful who they marry—"

"And that's so bad?" Wim said.

Hank clicked forward the carousel. Ila's right arm was lined with a half dozen perfect red tomatoes.

"It's class that's a bigger problem there, the class structure. It's so tight, it's unbreakable—"

"Like Holland once," Corrie said.

"We serve in a church of lower class people, not the really poor farmers but factory workers. No executives or professionals would ever set foot in our church. Beneath them to meet with our people."

The slide changed to a close-up of Tony sitting on his haunches, eyeing a tomato still hanging from the plant.

Wim poked Tony. "And who is that strange boy in your garden, Ila?"

The boy giggled on his grandfather's lap.

"That's nice tomatoes," Corrie said.

"So what is it—this class business that makes all the people down there so hungry for communism?" Wim said.

"It's very complex—what's going on there is very complex, Dad. Class is part of it, but it's a whole range of things. It's very difficult to explain, because everyone who criticizes isn't a Communist. Many Catholics are very critical, but they—"

"You can't be God-fearing and fight along with Communists. Don't try to tell me such things—"

Hank flashed a picture of Ila holding Tony. "Let's just skip it now, Dad. It's hard to explain. It's complex. Maybe some other time—"

"You think maybe your father can't understand?—"

"Of course not, Dad."

"I was so worried when Tony was born," Corrie said. "I didn't know what you had down there for a hospital, you know. If we was rich we would have sent you up here to be with us. But it was all okay?"

Ila told her it was just fine, perfectly clean. "Yankees think anything south of New Mexico is dirty, uncivilized, but it's not that way at all. Central America is very modern in parts. You wouldn't believe it. Americans and Europeans think everybody else isn't quite as cultured—"

"So what is it then, Hank, that makes communism look so good if already they aren't poor? They think it will make for them a better life?" Wim kept one arm around his grandson.

Hank wished he could hide in the comfort of the dark room.

"It's so easy for you to see Communists as enemies," Ila said. "We all think—I did too—that the biggest fight of all is American democracy against Russian communism. You can't help thinking that way here, Dad—it's in the air you breathe. But it's not that clear—it's not always that simple, I guess."

Hank spun the controls in his hand. He knew that his father was sitting back there seething, so he waited for a minute, Tony's little face up on the wall, because he wanted to show that he wasn't deliberately side-stepping the debate, avoiding a testimony on the conflict his father had always painted in lurid tones. Even though their views on certain issues frequently differed, he had inherited his father's vision of things, so he recognized it for what it was—a vast and intricate, perfect Dutch-Calvinist cobweb, infinite concentric circles hung on a system of tangents that originated in the man's creeds, a perfectly reasoned network of understanding into which every particle of God's creation—past, present, and yet to be discovered—had its own appointed place. Godless Marxists had their place somewhere near the SS slime who terrorized Holland during the last war. As long as a year ago Hank had begun to worry about the inevitability of this particular discussion.

"When you say that it's not so simple, Ila, then it's just like Hank would shut off that machine here in my mind—it's all darkness. I know and you know, too, what Marx thought of the Christian faith. And sometimes we hear in this country how there are men and women, under the banner of the Almighty, who help the Communists struggle against the government. You tell me now, how that makes sense, Hank—"

The wall turned into a broad meadow landscape with the faint charcoal lines of a mountain range barely visible against the horizon.

Hank waited for the picture to burn there for a time. "See those flowers there in the foreground," he said. "Those flowers grow like dandelions in some areas."

Corrie said they were beautiful.

At meals Wim Pietenpol was ritually quiet. He never spoke until the subject of conversation pleased him, or until he was convinced that he cared enough to take on an argument. So for fifteen minutes they sat around the Thanksgiving table, forking in yams and turkey, Ila telling Corrie how cooking wasn't all that much more trouble in El Salvador than it had been in America.

In the silence his father granted, Hank thought it was good to be at home, because he was sure that there was something fundamentally strong about spending holidays with relatives. After all, nothing undercut the family like the drive for social and geographical mobility, he thought. For seven years he and Ila had been away from families and roots. It was right and it was good for them to spend the holiday with his folks, even if it was only a weekend. Tony had never seen his grandparents before.

So together they sat there and ate.

"My father would say right now that this food must be good or else we'd find something to talk about." Wim repeated that line maybe a thousand times before, one of those jokes that Corrie and Hank had always chuckled about anyway, not because it was funny, but because they had never failed to laugh every time before, the old line as familiar as some old Sunday School chorus. Hank laughed because his father's repeating it reminded him of a pot full of memories—rolled roasts and baked chicken, eighteen years of meals around this table.

"So tell me, Dad," he said. "I haven't heard a word

about Easton yet. What's going on around here?" Hank passed his father the dinner rolls.

"What is there to say? When you get to our age, the only news is obituaries. Last year it was Ben Swart, but Corrie wrote you about that. This year—who now, once again? Corrie—who? I don't try to keep track."

Corrie busied herself mothering her grandson. Tony tried his best to handle a hill of mashed potatoes. "There was Chet Hartman—you remember, Wim—and the boy of Eernisse—"

"It was a terrible thing too. Hit by a train right here in the middle of town—"

"I remember you wrote about that one," Ila said.

"And your friend, your old friend Bill Sneider, Hank? You remember—Bill? He lost his father." Corrie took quick bites from her own plate between thrusts of peas at her grandson.

"Clarence Sneider. Is that right? It's hard to believe—"

"Cancer," Wim said.

"Really? Long time?"

Wim looked at his wife. "Two, maybe three years, Corrie? He was not in church for months—too weak. The man wasted away to nothing. Smoker, too. Always a cigarette poking out of his mouth."

"So where is Bill Sneider now?"

"Air Force, yet," Wim said.

"Is that right. Almost long enough to retire, I bet. Still flying?"

Wim pulled a napkin off his lap and scrubbed his mustache. "He flies, ja—he flies. But he doesn't fly home—"

"He was somewhere in Africa or Australia or something," Corrie said. "Couldn't come home for his father's funeral."

Years ago Hank's grandparents had always come over for Thanksgiving dinner, and that made it a big holiday. But mostly it was just the three of them. Hank and Corrie were already old when they had him, past 40.

Corrie would get out the dark brown tablecloth and the candles, and set the table the night before, as if the presence of the set table—silver on brown—would create the atmosphere as nicely as a Christmas tree. There was always turkey, and gravy, and sometimes pumpkin pie, because Wim and Corrie liked being American about some things. In Hank's mind Thanksgiving dinner was as much illusion as reality. To be here again seemed an odd kind of timeless dream, as if this dinner were the culmination of every dinner he had ever eaten, with the special tablecloth beneath his hands, with his father's long opening prayer. He had mislaid that memory for the last few years—the prayers. Wim's Thanksgiving prayers were really sermons. All Wim's public prayers were sermons, just like everything else that ever came from him. They were five minute admonitions to assess the family's blessings, to admit their total dependence on God, to find forgiveness for not doing precisely what he was warning them not to forget to do from here on out. Meanwhile, the food got cold.

"You see once when you get old like us, Ila; then you see if maybe that your big-time education you got can give you something else to think about than how many of your friends are gone and how many more are going," Wim said.

Ila laughed politely.

" 'What news?' my son says, and all I can think of is to show him on the church directory how many people we scratched out in the last year," he said. "Old people like us don't need social security—we need more pity, that's what we need."

Ila looked up at Hank. "Remember to wrap up some pity this Christmas, Hank. We'll save some money."

"And she cracks jokes too yet," Wim said, "this city girl."

Corrie dropped her fork, her eyes lit with a memory. "I remember now one thing I was going to tell you, Hank. Hector Laarman got remarried—"

"—she wasn't from Easton either, his new one," Wim said.

"—but they all say she is a good wife for him. From Collinsville."

"So who is Hector Laarman?" Ila said.

Corrie kept feeding Tony. "Hank used to love that man so much when he was a boy—"

"My first baseball coach," Hank said. He knew why his father sat quietly. "Hector was the kind of man that all the good people of town really didn't approve of. I remember he used to come to practice with a cigarette in his mouth and the smell of beer all over him. And he was divorced, maybe the only divorced man that I knew in town. It wasn't his fault either—you told me that, Mom. But he was a hero, you know. He was every Easton kid's hero." He swept a dinner roll through turkey gravy. "So he got himself married again, did he?"

"Why did you like him?" Ila said.

"It wasn't either that we didn't approve of him, Hank. Maybe it wasn't so good, we thought, for those little shavers to worship a man like Hector—"

"And he'd talk rough—use dirty language sometimes, I mean Easton dirty language."

"You liked him because he broke all the rules, is that it?" Ila helped herself to more turkey.

"Maybe just because he was the coach. Maybe that's all there was to it. I remember when he told us about the team we were going to be playing one Saturday—'they got a pitcher who's so gol darn big he can eat a bale of hay.' I can remember him saying that as if it was last week. I never heard an adult say 'gol darn.' Maybe sixth grade or so, that's how old I was."

Corrie shook her head. "Maybe it's a good thing we don't know everything that happens to a boy growing up," she said.

"Maybe he was the only adult who talked to us as if we were something more than kids," Hank said. The memory of the man settled Hank more where he sat.

Not quite a day had gone by since they had come home, and Hank couldn't help feeling that he was slowly descending a long ladder, closing in on something as firm as the earth itself. Today his father was happy, even lighthearted. Going to church together helped. They went on Thanksgiving morning. Corrie had said no, but Wim had insisted that he call the Pastor to remind him that his son, Hank, and the family, the missionary and his wife from El Salvador, would be in church that morning. So the Pastor made special mention of Hank and Ila Pietenpol and their little boy, back from the mission field. It made Hank proud to be introduced that way, because he knew that his father was happy, and proud too. Hank could feel that, even when they stood there in front while the whole church looked them over, judging to see how much hair he'd lost or whether Ila's figure had sagged after the baby. He could feel his father's pride through his father's blood in his own veins.

And his mother was taken completely by her only grandson. It was as if he and Ila might never have another. Corrie did everything for the boy. And Ila, her routine maternal responsibilities stolen by her mother-in-law, smiled and joked and teased as if she were for the first time trying to win her way into a family she had long ago been a part of. But Hank was still there on the ladder, closer to the bottom with every bite of Thanksgiving ritual. Maybe it was his own fault for not stepping down, standing up there on that ladder as if he were afraid to be at ease here, waiting instead for something to occur, something unforeseeable, something bothersome that was waiting to emerge from being home again after so many years.

Only a mother could whip such smooth potatoes.

"We got pie for dessert, so everybody leave room," Corrie said. "Tony want some ice cream, too?"

Tony shook his head.

Wim's fork scraped his plate, shrieking over the china. He twisted it upside-down and squeezed it between his lips. He was always finished first, even when they argued. To Wim, eating was simply a habit, a function of his physical self. Besides, once finished, he could sit back and supervise, one arm across his chest, the other one up with a tooth pick, poking little scraps of turkey from his teeth.

"So tell me once, Ila," he said, "what was the biggest adjustment for you down there in that other country?"

Ila sat there with her fork poised in front of her, her chin up. "Probably coming back," she said. She sat back and held her coffee in her hand, steam drifting up slowly. "Coming back," she said again, "the hardest kind of adjustment is coming back. It all seems so different now—once you've been gone."

Wim held his cup out to his wife.

"I mean, when you're away then you start to feel that home is really wonderful—you know, 'America!' When you're away from it, it seems so grand, so comfortable. I mean everything is new over there, and you hold on to a memory of what's familiar. You understand things by comparing—'it's not like this in Chicago.' 'In America it's not so humid.' 'The water's too sweet.' 'The nights are too hot.' You're always comparing at first, because it's all so different from what you know."

"It's like you remember only the good things about this country," Hank said. "When you're doing all these new things—shopping, eating—the old things seem so comfortable in your mind, like she says."

"And then coming back is kind of letdown, because your imagination has created this beautiful picture of how perfect life is in this country; after all—this is home." She sipped from her coffee. "And once you're back here, you wonder where home went, or even if it's really back in El Salvador."

"Some old men die—what else is it that's new to you here?" Wim said. "What's so much different here?"

Hank wasn't sure that Ila understood how thin the ice was. "Maybe it isn't new at all," he said. "Maybe nothing has changed about this country, about the way people live here." Hank pushed his chair back from the table and crossed his legs. "It's just that you hold up a memory of America for all those years and it gets to be fairytale like."

It was clear by Wim's face that he didn't understand. "So what's the matter with this country now?" he said.

"There's nothing really wrong with it—not when you say it that way, Dad," he said.

Wim's face stretched, pallid, vacant, as if he were for the time being transcending Thanksgiving and moving up into the roiling world of pure argument. Hank knew the look; it was as familiar as any of his father's age-old dinner jokes.

"She's not saying anything bad about this country," he said. "It's just that being away makes you see things differently."

"Don't tell me what I mean to say, honey," Ila said, turning to her father-in-law. "When you're not here, you start to see that there are other ways of looking at problems, at issues. You live in America, you think like an American. But it's different outside."

"So what are you now—after seven years—Americans or not?"

"We're Christians," Hank said. It ended the conversation as neatly as it evaded the question. It seemed like the perfect answer.

"And ice cream for Tony," Corrie said. "Say 'thank you,' Tony," she said.

The boy said thank you.

Wim was quiet again, forking in pumpkin pie lightly sprinkled with cinnamon.

"You think maybe my grandson will have a good school there?" Corrie pushed her chair around to face the boy.

Schools in El Salvador were, on the whole, better than the schools in the states, Ila told her. "Isn't that right, Hank?" she said.

Wim tried to appear preoccupied with the pie.

"Maybe it's because they don't tolerate misbehavior," Hank said. "Schools are tougher, it seems. They have much greater control in the classroom there."

Wim raised his eyes from the pie, then waited to speak until his mouth was cleared. "You know, Hank," he said, swallowing once more. "You know sometimes I think it's something like a sieve—the way you think about things, so full of holes." He pointed the fork. "I mean, you like it in the school—you like good strong discipline, but not in the government. When the government tries to keep order, then they call it repression. But in the school—and when it's your own boy—then it's got to be done." He rapped the fork down on the table. "With all that education you got I should think someone would have taught you how to think straighter."

"It's not the same, Dad," he said. "School and government aren't the same, just like children and adults aren't the same."

"You tell me once, you theologian, you tell me if sin is not the same—always working to destroy. You have naughty boys in school, and you have these disruptive groups in a society. For the good of the whole you must keep order. Isn't that the way it always is. And the body, it gets rid—"

"I've heard you say that a hundred times—guns and germs and all of that—"

"A hundred times?"

"At least—"

"Then you got no excuse at all for being so foolish."

There were times when anything his father said was like a final, resounding amen, the times when he hated the just-whipped retreat he'd force himself into. In San Salvador, he'd been the American preacher for seven years, the final authority on everything for a hundred people. But here it was always the insufferable kowtow, as if he were some dog forever getting caught for dirtying the carpet. And this man who was nothing but his father was always standing up in front of him like some fuhrer with a Bible.

Finally, giving in to him spread a measure of peace around the proverbed dining room, settled the needle-work aphorisms, and while the sheer force of his will bullied Hank's self-image, he knew—twenty years of meals in this room had taught him—that self-denial was the Christian way, humility, turning-the-other-cheek, "the meek shall inherit the earth."

"Tony want some more ice cream?" Corrie said.

Hank laid his fork on the pie plate and retrieved the crumbs from the tablecloth, his mother's best tablecloth, the deep brown cloth with embroidered edges. Maybe the tablecloth was the closest his parents would ever come to royalty.

Corrie brought Tony some more ice cream, and she handed her husband the Bible with her right hand.

Wim licked his thumb as his fingers played through the thin pages of the Bible. "I think maybe this one would be good on Thanksgiving. You remember, Corrie, how this was the one that we would read during the Depression?" He looked up over his glasses. "You and Ila don't remember that—the Depression. Maybe, I think it would be good for you to have to go through something like that, for your whole generation."

Corrie wound her arm around her grandson. "Ach, this man I married, sometimes he says things that are so foolish. What kind of man wishes the Depression on people he loves? Thank God it is over once and for all."

Wim stopped paging and looked at his wife, then at Ila. " 'Helpmeet' the Bible calls her, but sometimes I think that maybe the word means something like a conscience." He laughed at his own joke.

"Forty years of conscience, Dad, I would think that you would learn," Ila told him, with a playful smile that nudged any disrespect out of the straight line of her irony.

Wim pointed at his son. "You got one there too, Hank," he said.

He read from Habakkuk, chapter three. " 'Though the fig tree will not blossom, and there be no fruit on the vines; though the yield of the olive should fail and the fields produce no food; though the flocks should be cut off from the field, and there be no cattle in the stalls, yet will I exult in the Lord, I will rejoice in the God of my salvation. The Lord is my strength.' "

"You remember, Corrie?" he said, closing the book.

Corrie nodded.

He asked Hank to give thanks. "So—will my son the preacher pray for us?"

He knew his father didn't mean it that way—pray for us—as if he were supposed to perform a prayer. He consented, only because he didn't dare refuse, even though he wasn't inspired to pray at that very moment, still prickling with humiliation and something he rather stubbornly recognized as self-pity. But he prayed anyway, because prayer came almost instinctively to him after so many years, sitting again in this chair, in this roomful of his mother's moralisms. And it was nothing at all to arrange the old phrases, fuse them with thees and thous, and roll on for several minutes without even engaging his mind in the process. "We thank You, Lord, for the abundance of blessings which Thou hast showered upon us." Almost instinctively he straightened his back. "Help us to remember those who are not so fortunate as we are, some whose very life is upheld by a slice of bread or a bowl of rice." He paused for a moment, just long enough to underline the sentiment with silence. Prayer was a podium after all; his father had long ago taught him as much. "And forgive us in this country for our waste. Help us to remember our starving brothers and sisters in the poor nations of the world. Help us not to forget—"

Later, Wim said it was a good prayer. "Thank you," he said. He poked his fork at the turkey for one last bite.

"I'm glad that you prayed after the meal," he said. "It wouldn't have tasted so good if you had said all of that before." He stared at his son, as if to call him out into battle again.

Hank wanted no part of it.

"You think I should be sorry that I have a good house here and enough food, Hank? Is that what you want?"

"Of course not—"

"You think maybe we can't have a Thanksgiving without guilt?" he said.

Corrie and Ila picked up plates from the brown tablecloth.

Wim carried the church projector down to his basement while the women cleaned up upstairs. Corrie lived on the ground floor of the old house—the plaques and the Bavarian landscape, the dustless knick-knacks turned the place into her home. But Wim, ever since he had retired from the factory, spent his waking hours in the basement workshop. Nothing had ever been finished off in the basement, the exposed rafters crossing the ceiling like steps, the gray block walls lined with rough mortar edges. Naked light bulbs hung from between the rafters on thick black cords, and the floor was cold concrete, except for one worn throw rug at the workbench. As always, everything was cleanly swept.

"Look at this here once, Hank," his father said, removing the plate that covered the controls of the projector. "Look here at this mess."

Dust grew over the insides like a fine mold.

"That's the death of machinery," he said. "Dust is the death of machinery."

"Think you can fix it?"

Wim looked up at his son. "What you think? I spend thirty years in the salvage shop for nothing? You always was too much like your mother in some things, Hank.

You know what you pay for when you bring something like this into the shop—you pay twenty dollars an hour, maybe more today, and you pay for your own stupidity, that's all. You pay somebody to do what you don't want to learn. You think them guys are smart for fixing these things? None of them have college, Hank—no sir."

Hank looked over the plywood sheets stacked against the wall, perpendicular to his father's workbench. "Hasn't changed much down here, Dad," he said.

"Church equipment this is. Nobody watches church equipment because they all have higher callings. Friday night, you know, you have to show the church your slides."

Sores lined his father's forearms, nicks and bumps from the workshop maybe, round, half-healed sores, as if his age spots had peeled back his skin and left red blotches, some the size of dimes. Hank saw them when Wim rolled up his sleeves. Sores always healed slower on old people, riding in the thin folds of wrinkled skin or slowly crusting away on a wrist, staying there for months it seemed, until finally the soft and pink scar turned leathery orange like the rest of the skin. The sores were new to Hank, coming through his father's skin like some alien chemical from his bloodstream or like a long-repressed memory finally becoming real. Wim was an old man. He was an old man with marred skin.

A long fluorescent light hung over the width of the bench. Old steel rings hung from between the rafters, bits of corroded iron and tin were stuck into dark corners in the cubby-holes above the bench, and shards of metal poked out of coverless cigar boxes. And the gun case stood there now, downstairs; it used to be next to the stairs on the main floor.

"You stopped smoking, Dad?" Hank said. Years ago, in the corner, a half pound coffee can stood, usually choked with fat, burned-out cigar butts stewing in their own ash.

"Corrie says it's a dirty habit. After forty years, she

says she thinks maybe she would be happier if I quit."
He pulled out a tiny screwdriver and poked in the insides of the projector. "Now always I have to worry that I'll live too long, that she'll go before me, and then here I'll sit without her or a cigar."

He sat, as always, on the stool, his shoulders slightly slumped so his suspenders slackened and his chest seemed to disappear. He nodded as he worked, because nodding was a kind of habit with him, as if he were constantly approving things like some master of quality control.

"So what have you been working on lately?" Hank said.

"You want to see?"

"Of course."

"I don't do so important work as my son, but look at this." He pulled a black bicycle footpump from beneath the bench, fixed the end of the hose to a nozzle mounted to the frame of some invention, slapped his toe on the pump, and shot long gulps of air into the little machine. Tiny red wheels turned in perfect silence, as cylinders, round as quarters, pumped up and down smoothly, as if they were bobbing in oil. "It's quite a thing, eh? I made it all from scratch, from old stuff, down here."

"That's really something, Dad."

"Ja, it's pretty good too, I guess." He kept shoving air into the little engine, the red wheels circling noiselessly. "It's not easy either, you know, all those parts. But even this old toolmaker will tell you that there's nothing in this world that's perfect—oh no." He popped the nose of the nozzle, and tucked the pump back under the bench.

"Sometimes I carve too. Corrie likes me to make these birds." He pointed toward the corner where three wooden birds, their thin necks straight, their long beaks pointing straight into the sky, were propped. "It's getting so I can make one almost finished in one afternoon. People buy them too sometime. It's hard to believe. See this one," he said. He flipped one over, his hand around the neck. "Wim P.," it said, and the date.

"On the lathe you make these?" Hank said.

"You can't make such a thing on a lathe, Hank. Here, look at this." He slid a homemade box full of carving knives from beneath metal grooves he had mounted under the bench.

"You're keeping busy then?"

"A man who works with his hands—retirement is only the beginning for him." He stuck the bird back in the corner. "You take one of these along for Ila maybe," he said. "Before you leave, you take one." Wim leaned back on his stool, looking into the guts of the projector.

Hank ran his finger around the cylinders of his father's little engine. "So you've got your guns down here now. Ma tell you to get them out of her upstairs, I suppose?"

"She said it was silly for a man so old to have guns around. As if we had no faith or something."

Only the severity of clear Biblical injunction had served to restrain Corrie from long ago pawning her husband's guns. "Woman—obey thy husband"—such words, fraught as they were with hellfire, barely stifled her distaste for a sport she considered in one condemning breath both "barbaric" and "American." Hank had felt the sharp limits of her tolerance early, from the time he was old enough to understand that the sober man who sat across from him at Saturday night's supper—the man who considered so piously the obligations of proper Sabbath observance in both his opening prayer and the supper conversation—this man was not the hunter in the plaid coat whose steps he'd followed all afternoon, the man whose waist was hung with a belt half-full of shotgun shells, the man whose cold-pinched face lit up nonetheless when a pheasant, flushed from standing corn, froze in mid-air and went down in one shot.

They never talked hunting upstairs, never cleaned their guns in front of her, never carted in the game before it had been thoroughly cleaned, before it bathed in brine in the one steel pan Corrie allowed them for their birds. Wim talked hunting only in his basement workshop. The Apostle Paul commanded Corrie to live with her husband's guns, but through so many years of marriage she had worked out an unsteady compromise—I'll live with guns if I don't ever have to hear about them.

"Why don't you just get rid of them, Dad? You're not hunting anymore, really, are you?" He turned the latch on the case and pulled out a rifle.

"Because you and me are going Saturday," he said. "First day for deer. Since August I been watching on the ridge—maybe you remember there, on the road straight down to the lake—and every time on Saturday morning they're out on the trail, a big one too, some others and maybe some does. So you and me will go, like years past. I know where they will be. Here and there on trees you see where the big one scrapes his antlers. They will be there. I got it planned, Hank—right where you will stand. I got it planned already."

Hank said being back in the old woods sounded good.

"He's out there too; he's out there waiting for us, that big one. Maybe this year we get him." He pulled his glasses from behind his ears and rubbed the bridge of his nose with his fingers.

"I don't even have a license—"

"So what is a license? Gerrit Franken goes to our church. He'll arrest you if one morning you come out to the woods with your father?"

"It's not legal without—"

"All these years I pay my taxes here, and one morning when my son comes home, I can't take him out to the woods with me?"

Hank snapped out the bolt of the rifle and pointed the barrel. Light circled down the rifling. His father's guns were always clean. Half the joy had been anticipa-

tion, the jitters of the night before, knowing that sometime in the darkness his father would come to his bed-
side and shake him, his father's hands on the small of his
back, rocking him awake. And then out. A silent breakfast. A night full of stars. Cold against his face. The
woods, perfectly dark. It was a ritual with his father.
Pheasants were one thing, but Wim Pietenpol had never
shot a deer, not once. He never claimed the opportunity.

"You still can handle one of these, you think? Maybe
too long you been a preacher?" His softest laughter was
most cutting; it had an intimidating edge honed by un-
derstatement, like a finger between the ribs: "ha, ha, ha,
isn't this funny what I'm saying?"

"Maybe you should have a gun down there in that
country with all the guerrillas. How about it—you take
one along when you go back?" Wim pulled on his glasses
and turned back to the projector.

"It'd be silly for me to take—"

"It's not silly to have a gun, Hank. I know that. When
the Communists come—first they take the guns, you
know. You have Cubans there in that country now, don't
you? And now you have a family to protect. I don't have
to tell you about the Communists and what they do to
people."

"Guns are an American disease, Dad. People don't
have guns in other countries, not like here. It would
look as if—"

"And you should worry about what it looks like?
With the Communists there you have more to worry
about."

"Besides, I'd never get it in. They'd throw me back to
the States—"

"What kind of place is it that would keep guns out of
the hands of good people?"

"It's only in this country that people think they need
guns. People aren't that stupid anywhere else."

When his father turned away from the projector,
Hank knew he had said too much, that he had inched

over the line that kept argument back from simple conversation, that now his father's mind was gathering wits
for an offensive. His quietness gave it away; the lull was
only temporary. Wim stared at the sores on his arms.

"Seven years away from your father and now you
come back to me a Communist," he said, still deliberately understated to hide the attack behind poking fun.

"Come on, Dad—"

"So what is it you do down there? Do you tell those
people that they are oppressed? You tell them maybe it's
better to rebel so they can get for themselves more
money? Is that it?" He turned back to the machine again,
as if the guise of working would make his words more
conversational, less deliberately chosen and less condemning. "And then all of us here—the dumb ones who
don't have college—all of us are thinking all the time
that you're preaching the Word, but you aren't—you
aren't preaching the Word, only the love of money—"

"You don't understand—"

"What do you mean, 'don't understand?' You think
for one minute that rebellion and money will do for
those people anything eternal? So what have you done
for them? When you leave, what have you done?—"

"They're more than souls, Dad. Just like you and
me—we're more than souls—"

"And all that education. We don't send you to school
for all the education and then want you to side with
Communists. Where do you get that, Hank?—those
ideas? You get that at seminary?"

"You aren't listening, Dad. You're just talking—"

"Once the seminary goes, then the whole church
goes."

"Dad—"

"And pretty soon we lose the Scripture too. Modernists. We all be modernists and the church is an empty
cave. Nothing in there anymore but crying women—"

At the beginning he'd always have that silly smile on
his face, the false grin deliberately drawn to dramatize

that the opening rounds were little but maneuvering. Hank hated the smile he had almost forgotten, hated it as if he had never spent seven years thousands of miles from his father, as if this basement battle was simply another in a lifelong, uninterrupted series—yesterday's, today's, tomorrow's.

"Dad," he said, "listen to me."

His father's deliberate silence surprised him, and he fumbled for words, his rifle still in his hands. "You can't treat people as if you are running some salvage shop—this one saved, throw it in the bin—that one wrecked, stick it in here. We're talking about people, and you can't handle them as if they have no bodies and no future and no minds. My goodness—" He leaned the gun back up in the rack.

"So then you tell them to rebel against the government. 'Kill off the dirty rulers,' you tell them. 'Spread that corruption around a little so everybody gets his share.' You tell me where in Christ's gospel I can find that message. You show me sometime." When he twisted his head up at Hank, the fake smile was gone.

"We are called to do justice—"

" 'Do justice,' you say. Justice in my Bible is a cup of water to the thirsty, not a pocketful of money or a cup of blood. 'Blessed is the man who walks not in the counsel of the ungodly or stands in the way of sinners.' You sit with Communists and then forever you will sit and wonder why the Lord doesn't bless your work in El Salvador."

"You can't treat flesh and blood people as if they are nothing but souls."

"So what does it mean to *treat?* The church calls you to *preach,* not to *treat.* Doctors, maybe, we send to *treat*—not preachers—"

Silence. They never really stopped, these arguments. They covered themselves for a while with quietness, the way a child buries his feet in beach sand. Wim turned back to the projector, back to the redemption of work.

After the fights, silence and guilt arrived simultaneously in Hank's mind, at the same moment Wim went back to his tools. He worked busily, as if they hadn't even spoken in the first place. Work always intensified the silence and the guilt, as if physical labor were some magic cure, as if talk and the argument had somehow disrupted creation and led to all the anger, anger which made them forget that work was what they should have been about in a world that belonged to God. Hence the guilt.

"I can't ever win an argument with you, Dad," Hank said. "I can't ever win anyway, but I just can't stop trying either."

Wim plugged in the projector and the fan started.

"I don't want to fight. Sunday already we're going. I don't want to fight with you—"

Wim blew out the dust and wiped the screwdriver on the apron hung from the bench. "When to me it is clear that my only son is wrong, then my Lord commands that I say it," he said.

Hank heard his own son's feet slap on the kitchen floor above them.

T W O

"Why is it that when I'm with him I always feel as if I'm walking on a ledge somewhere?" Hank said.

Side by side, they lay together, motionless, in the double bed Wim had bought at an auction when Hank had called home from college to announce his engagement.

The bed was in his own room, the room he'd slept in as a child, except there always had been a single bed before.

"It's the way he is," Ila said.

"Do you feel it too, or is it just me?"

"He's always trying to draw you into a fight or something." She turned toward him. "Always preaching. Always was, that I can remember." She draped her arm over his chest. "Maybe he loves you too much."

"Fighting is part of him—that's what he told me once. Fighting is the Dutch part, fighting the union at work, fighting for orthodoxy—'I have fought the good fight'— always fighting. It's like breathing."

"But why fight you?" she said.

"You'd figure he'd think he already won this one, wouldn't you? I mean, my goodness, his son is a missionary. I don't think he could have wanted any more from me. You'd think he could settle back and let me live. He's won the big one."

She pulled her hands behind her head, elbows out. "It's not in him to let up, Hank."

"So he's got to keep pushing me, always pushing me, as if he can sanctify me with his own grace." He pulled his hands up to his face, rubbing his eyes. "I remember when I was just a kid, he used to take his hand and lay it on my forehead, like this—" He put a hand up in the air, curving his fingers as if he were holding a melon.

"What do you mean?" Ila said.

"Like this." He pulled himself up on his elbow and reached for her. "Like a faith healer. And he'd just leave it there on my forehead, you know, for a minute or so. Before I went to sleep he'd do it."

"Odd feeling," she said, pulling his hand away.

"I used to love it. It was like his kiss. Security, maybe—I don't know. I can feel it yet, you know, his hand, his palm right here on my forehead. He'd stop me from crying."

Ila squeezed his arm. "Just try to stay away from a big

fight, honey. We'll be here only a couple days, and I don't think Mom can take a big brawl. I know I can't."

Only wallpapered plaster separated them from Wim and Corrie, and they could hear his low voice, garbled and indistinct, as if the sound were being carried through a torn speaker.

"I'd give anything to hear what they're saying," Hank said.

Ila turned over on her stomach and tucked her body next to his. "I hate this bed," she said. "I always have. It's so blame soft."

He turned towards her. "When we were first married you never complained," he said. He laid his hand on the back of her neck.

"Why is it that whenever you say, 'when we were first married'—it sounds like nostalgia to me. I don't like that."

"Age, my dear," he said. "All those olden days start appearing in sepia-tone once you pass thirty."

"Then it's relative, at least. When we're fifty, some night you'll say, 'Remember the night we lay together in the crummy bed at Dad's house and talked about old times?' Then today will be the good old days." She turned away from him. "So the difference between nostalgia and plain old memory is only a matter of years."

He ran his hand slowly up the middle of her back. "Depends, I suppose, on what happens on a given night that's memorable."

"You're not kidding now?" she said.

"What does that mean?"

She pulled her arms beneath her and propped herself up on her elbows. Ila, he thought, controlled the dramatic pause more artistically than any seminary orator. She lay there, half-reclining, staring into the headboard as if some revelation were about to appear in the wood grain. "I mean, every time—"

"Shhh—" he said.

She whispered. "—every time you get here in this bed you go honeymoon crazy."

"You mean to say you can remember seven long years ago here?"

"I won't forget this crummy bed so easily," she said. "My husband is one thing, but this bed isn't a whole lot more than a hammock."

"It's not nostalgia, then?"

She dropped her head between her outstretched arms and inhaled, as if the answer were some painful revelation. "There's nothing at all nostalgic about this bed," she said, "and I've never been away from my husband long enough to grow wistful—much less nostalgic." She faced him. "And don't misinterpret that." She jammed her knuckles into his ribs.

"What's that for?" he said.

She put her hand on the headboard. "Do you realize that if I could punch my fist through the wall, I'd probably conk your dad on his head?"

Hank thought it was funny. "What is the big deal, Ila?"

"In this bed I'm nothing but some adolescent fantasy of yours." She punched him again.

"Hey—"

She clamped her hand over his mouth. "Listen," she said. "I think it's Dutch—I think they're speaking Dutch because they're sure we're listening to them."

He pulled her hand away.

"I don't even hear them," he said.

"Well, aren't you the liberated one?" She lay perfectly flat. "You know, sometimes I think it's dark in this bedroom only because your father's shadow is up here hovering over us."

He hugged her, his right arm over her back. "So what's wrong with this bed?" he said.

On Friday morning the gray sky was full of lake snow, but Hank wanted to go to the lakeshore anyway, like the old days—just to stand there and feel the old rush of cold, damp air heaving up from the broad belt of water running in both directions to the very corners of the horizon. The fishermen were gone by November, as were the city people that lived out tranquil summers in the row of cottages set back up on the ridge of sand off the beach. The sand was smooth and dry and trackless, spotted with pebbles and stones swept up by the wind.

"It's not much to look at now, all of this, not by Thanksgiving." Wim lit his cigar in the brush of the lake breeze.

"I thought you said you stopped, Dad," Hank said.

"At home," Wim said. He kept the pipe cupped in his glove. "Mainly it's the gulls and the wind that's here now. But you remember, Hank. Years ago you spent half your life out here." He kicked at the stones in the sand, small stones, round and flat as coins. He reached down slowly, bending only at the knees, and picked up several. "Tony watch Grandpa," he said.

Hank held his son's gloved hand and watched as the old man's scrawny legs carried him down from the ridge. He trudged through the dry sand down to the shore line, fingering a stone as round as a cookie. Wim looked back at them to be sure he had an audience, then he tried to skip the stone off the unruly surface water, choppy swells just angry enough to whitecap. The stone slipped perfectly into the water.

"The lake's too rough, Dad," Hank yelled. "You can't skip stones."

"Come here, Tony," Wim said, waving the boy down with his fist full of flat stones.

In October they would come out to the beach together in the dark of early morning—five, maybe earlier—and pull on chest-high waders. Duck season. The trunk would be full of decoys and ropes and silvery lead weights, melted toothpaste tubes. He couldn't see the water when the sky was overcast, and the press of cold against his thighs seemed a threat, a nether world schooled with huge, ugly carp hanging motionless in dark and thick morning waves, eyeing his bottom half. It was silly to be afraid and even then he knew it. But fear was burrowed deeper than reason could reach, and just knowing there was nothing to fear couldn't warm the chill that shook his fingers. Maybe it was wading, walking through waist-deep water without seeing your feet beneath you. And then, the sky beginning to glow, seeing that stump of upper-body next to him spreading decoys, just the sight of the man would rub the fear into excitement, his father out there with him. A few years later they had a skiff—tiny little thing—when Wim got sick of not being able to call those lake ducks all the way into shore. But always it would be only the two of them out in the heavy dampness, Wim always instructing, always talking.

Wim collected stones for his grandson, and Tony chucked them out into the surf, a sidearm fling, elbow locked, as if he were a miniature olympian with a discus.

"It's too rough, Dad. You can't make 'em skip," Hank yelled.

Wim seemed not to hear him in the rustle of waves breaking over each other.

Hank took long steps through the dry sand down to the shore.

"I think this boy will be a ball-player," Wim said, "maybe better than his father was." He pointed. "Look at that arm."

"Soccer," Hank said. "In El Salvador, he'll play soccer."

His father nodded as if it made no difference. He looked timeless in his old red plaid hunting coat.

"I was thinking about duck hunting, Dad. You remember? All those decoys, you know—early in the morning?"

"Ja, you remember that boat we had, that little one?" Wim kept tossing out stones, sidearm, like his grandson, and the wind kept flipping them over once before they would slip into the waves without as much as a ripple.

"We strapped that boat on the car, that little thing, huh? Oh, your mother hated that thing. She was scared."

"She never acted scared," Hank said.

"You think you know everything that goes on when you're growing up. Here," he pointed at Tony, "this little one won't know everything what goes on always with you and Ila. Thank the Lord he won't. What does the Psalmist say in number 73—'if I would have told you all what I was thinking, I would have ruined the generations yet to come'—I can't quote the Scriptures any more so good like I could once. Maybe in the Dutch yet. But there is some things that you don't know, Hank, some things we never told you." He seemed distanced suddenly. "But I was saying—Ma hated that boat, you know. Oh, she was scared for us."

"With good reason—"

"Sure with good reason. This big lake you don't want to fool with—like the sea in Holland. You don't fool with her—not with that little skiff we had. Waves get angry, the wind changes—you get off quick. You don't fight with God's nature."

He stopped for more stones. Tony scrambled over to his grandfather to reload. Hank knew the boy wasn't thinking of him, not with his grandfather chucking stones, chucking stones and lecturing, always lecturing, everything coming out a lecture, as if Hank were forever an undergraduate.

"You remember the first time out on that thing. We took her out, what, maybe 200 yards, maybe less, and dropped in some decoys. Then we waited, and pretty soon the ducks come? Black ducks or some ugly ducks, lake ducks—skinny ones full of seaweed. And you, up with the gun on your shoulder. 'Hank,' I says, 'you wait now once till they get in range.' You remember that time, Hank?"

Hank remembered.

"You think back once. 'You wait till those ducks get in close,' I says. 'Don't go shooting out the sky.' So here

they come, and bam! bam! bam! you let them have it
with that pump. And those things keep right on flying,
huh? Not one duck. 'You missed,' I says to you."
"I thought it was the gun." Hank could feel that new
pump yet in his hands.
" 'Them ducks are way out of range,' I says to you
then. 'No sir,' you say. 'Not with this choke I got here.'
You think you're so smart with that new pump. And
you're mad at me too yet. And the sun is coming up
there—all that orange between the clouds." He pointed
to a colorless horizon.
"My son knows everything—that's what he thinks.
You didn't know the big lake plays tricks. You remember
that, Hank?"
"Sure, I remember," Hank said.
Wim raised his arms and pointed out into the waves,
both hands in front, with two fingers. "When you shoot
on the lake you got to look at things different than when
you are on land, because there's nothing that's out there
to help you see the distance right. You remember what I
told you?"
Hank fell to his haunches to pick some stones from
the sand.
"You got no perspective—you got no trees between
you and the ducks. You got nothing to judge distance."
He pivoted to face Hank, like a sergeant might have
turned, his eyes bright, as always, with a sense of firmly
staked truth. "Those scrawny lake ducks are out of
range almost fifty yards. They just laugh it off."
"Grandpa," Tony said, pulling at his grandfather's
coat. Wim gathered more stones.
Hank kicked through the small stones. "It's too rough
to skip stones, Dad." he said.
"Here now, Tony, like this." Wim circled a stone with
his finger, and spun it out into the lake. "So what, Hank?
So what if it won't skip in the waves? Tony don't know
any different."
In high school, Hank once had the thought that his

father's veins carried red ink. Things hadn't changed at
all—from the blue-gray clouds, tipping with moisture,
hanging above the horizon like some half-drawn curtain,
to the windswept sand banks and the sharp beach grass.
And his father was still here, part of the lakeshore landscape. Only Tony was new. Tony was here now to remind him that fifteen years of his life with Wim Pietenpol were already behind him somewhere, years without
the lakefront, without hunting. Tony's pudginess proved
that somewhere in El Salvador's capital city a church
stood in a poor community, next to a house called their
home. Without Tony he felt in danger of falling into a
deep cast of childhood, his childhood, a world that
seemed at once fearfully enclosed and eternally safe.

"See those clouds, Hank?" Wim said. "Lake snow
coming, maybe a couple inches. Perfect for hunting deer.
Perfect for the first day down here." He started back up
the beach, leaving footsteps that drew like an old path, a
wake as forceful as a magnetic field. And it angered
Hank to know that his father simply assumed his only
son, the missionary, would follow him up and away from
the lake's edge.

"Tonight you have to speak at church," Wim said.
"You can come back again sometime."

"I want you all to know," he announced after the
slides were shown, "that my father made this all possible." He spoke from center aisle of the church, the
remote control of the slide projector in his right hand, a
mike clipped to his tie. "My father—on Thanksgiving
Day nonetheless—fixed this machine."

People laughed when they heard it, knowing Wim
Pietenpol as they did. Maybe there were two hundred,
including children in the pews, most of them up front, a
row of kids in the first row close to the screen. Behind
the kids sat Ila and his parents.

"Now," he said, "maybe some of you have a few questions."

One of the children wanted to know if there was Christmas in El Salvador. The crowd chuckled. And another wondered what kind of animals the people hunted in the forests on the pictures.

Then the pastor raised his hand. "Hank," he said, "what do you make of this 'liberation theology?' "

Hank lifted the carousel off the projector. "Pastor Van Gaalen asks what I make of this 'liberation theology?' " he said, repeating the question for those who might not have heard. He placed the tray in its own yellow box.

In the front row the children were becoming impatient, fidgety, after the long sit in the dark.

"I haven't had a tough question like that since my licensing exam," he said, and the older folks laughed. One of his father's hands was locked over the pew in front of him. "Generally," he said, "liberation theology is the means by which some missionaries see the nature of their work. They see their work as a ministry to what they might call 'the whole man.' They ridicule attempts at preaching Christ when there is no simultaneous push to raise the social and economic levels of the people in any country." He loosened his tie, hearing the rustle of kids in the front row. It was a question which wouldn't hold their interest.

Pastor Van Gaalen gave him a tentative smile. "But what do you think?" he said.

"My role is to preach the gospel," he said, "but I have some sympathies with Christians who might be following what they call 'liberation theology.' " It was safe, he felt.

When he looked for more questions, his father's hand stretched across the sanctuary.

"I think these kids up here have about had enough." He smiled at the fidgeters. "You're all getting anxious for those cookies out there, aren't you?"

"One more yet," his father said.

Hank heard the crowd chuckle at his father's persistence.

"I got one," Wim said.

"So who am I to say no to my own father?" he said, and the light laughter warmed.

"Is it true that some so-called missionaries have used the gospel to preach communism?"

He lifted the first box of slides atop the other, squaring the corners perfectly.

"My father wonders if some missionaries are actually Communists," he repeated. He looked up and smiled. "I have no knowledge of any missionary who is using Christianity to work for Communist takeover anywhere in Central America."

He turned back to the kids, trying to engage their attention.

"But is it true what we hear," his father said, "that this 'liberation theology' seeks revolution and a Communist state? This is true, Hank—yes or no?"

Even the kids sensed the sudden intensity of the question in the way the people waited for his answer. It was as if they understood that something odd was happening.

"My father wonders whether 'liberation theology' and socialism are often linked as cultural forces," he said. He pulled the cord out from the back of the projector and started winding it around his fist. "I can't say yes or no to a question like that, because the answer is so complex. Maybe afterward if some of you would like to know more— But it's really not so easy to separate issues as you might like to think in the States." He glanced down at the cord, wound the plug into the knot of wires, and laid it on the piano bench they used for a stand.

He saw his father's hand, but he deliberately looked away, twisted the wire from his tie, and held the mike out in front of him. "Perhaps Pastor Monsma will offer closing prayer," he said.

When his folks went to bed, he told Ila that he didn't want to go hunting with his father early the next morning.

"Hunting?" she said.

"First day of deer season. Didn't I tell you about him asking me?"

She said she thought it would be silly for him to go deer hunting if he really didn't want to go. "Besides," she said, "what are we going to do with a deer anyway?" She paged through a church magazine, barely scanning the pages. They sat at the opposite ends of the couch.

"It's not really to get one," he said. "My father never shot a deer—not in twenty-five years. It's not really to shoot a deer. It's just to be out there."

"Why risk getting killed?" she said.

He stood, then walked to the front window. "I don't think he could shoot a deer really. It's not that he doesn't see them either. My father knows those lake-shore woods like nobody else." He drew back the front curtain with his hands. "Perfect day tomorrow, too. Lake snow. Perfect for opening day. Maybe I should go—you know, for him."

"So what did you tell him?" Ila said.

"He's leaving at five. I told him if I wasn't up, I wouldn't be going."

She laid the open magazine upside-down over the arm of the couch. "He'll be let down if you don't go with, I suppose?"

He pulled at the drapes, then drew the cord. "You know, it's funny. For the last seven years I've been so far away from him—it's almost as if he really doesn't exist anymore." He looked through the open windows. "And then you come back home to his old world here—this home—and it seems so real that everything else, even our own church, seems like a vacation. I mean all of El Salvador—it seems dreamlike." He hung his fingertips on the lattice work of the front window. "I think it was just last year sometime—I don't remember exactly—but

I still wrote down this address—this house and this town—as my permanent address."

"When does that stop?" Ila had her hands up behind her head, pulling up the loose hair out of her neck.

"When they're finally gone, I suppose." A light mist formed at the bottom edge of the window pane. He pushed his finger through it, making tears against the glass. "Look at that snow out there. Coming straight down, like Currier and Ives." He turned back to her. "Like to take a walk in the snow?"

"I've been away too long. Looks just cold to me," she said, pulling her feet beneath the quilted housecoat she borrowed from her mother-in-law.

"I don't know," he said. "I think I'd go with him if I really knew why I wanted to go—if I knew it wasn't just to please him again. I've spent half my life pleasing him." He put his hands in his pockets.

"Spite is no reason to stay home. What do you want to do, Hank? You really feel like going along?"

"I'm not so sure I know. If I go, it's to please him—if I don't, it's to spite him."

Ila shrugged her shoulders and picked up the magazine once again.

"I don't even have a license," he said. "It's against the law."

He heard his father leave, but he couldn't get back to sleep. He looked around the room at the strip of decorative paper where the walls met the ceiling—saddles, ten-gallon hats, branding irons, and six guns in an eternal pattern. He could barely make them out in the darkness. American West. An immigrant Hollander and his wife decorate their boy's room with the American West. He could barely make out the designs in the darkness. His father had glued it up there when he was a little boy like Tony, so long ago he could barely remember. The string of Western images looked silly, the boy in the room already long gone, but Wim and Corrie never thought much about taking it down or remodeling—only Ila and himself ever slept in the old room. Years ago he himself had pulled down the faded pennants.

"Why don't you just go?" Ila said. "Take our car. You know where he is, don't you?"

The way she turned over, he knew she was angry with him, annoyed probably, that he was awake in the dark in the middle of the night, arguing with himself.

"You awake?" he said.

She spoke without raising her head. "Some night when it's terribly hot, you'll wake up and tell yourself that you should have gone," she said. "Go on."

The snow fell straight down from the sky, flakes big and slow as ticker-tape. Hank found his father's car on the lake road where he knew it would be parked, maybe an inch or so of snow in a blanket over the hood and top, with two short humps where Wim had flashed the wipers over the windshield. There was a truck there and another car down the road. He guessed there were other hunters.

The woods were dark, the road a wide slat of gray between the ditches, white with heavy snow. But he'd done this before, come out to the woods and trudged through the darkness. He'd done it many times before. Years ago, even before he was in high school, awake in the early morning darkness of his room, his youthful nerves running a stream of sparks through his fingers. Those were the great moments of his boyhood, walking along quietly in the reverence his father held for the great God of the forest.

He walked to the side of the road and saw his father's boot tracks in the snow. The forest hid the eastern sky, but he guessed it would be some time before the daylight would spread through the trees.

He remembered the first time he had seen an animal die. That was here, in these woods, in mid-winter. They were coming back from something—he couldn't remember what—when the car had struck an opossum. It was hunting season, and Wim had his rifle in the trunk. They stopped immediately and searched for the animal.

"Look at this," his father had said, pointing a flashlight into the ditch.

He had been just a boy. The opossum writhed in the long grass, its black legs smashed by the car. A snarling mouth and two eyes, red as berries in the beam of light. His father gave him the flashlight, aimed, and squeezed the trigger of the old .22. The shot was muffled, almost silenced. Then they stood there, waiting for the motion to cease.

The animal pawed at its forehead, at the perfect hole between its eyes, as if somehow it could scratch out the lead. "Possum," his father had said, as if it were some eulogy. "Some things maybe we would rather not have to see."

It had taken too long for the black paws to stop their frantic scratching.

He kept walking into the woods, following his father's carefully placed tracks. Wim had avoided certain spots, even certain trees he knew would shed noisy twigs. The waffle print was easy to follow, even in the darkness.

Years ago, on Sunday afternoons they would go together to the woods, no guns, just a honey bucket with some coffee, and two white cups—maybe a couple of slices of bread. "You find for us a nice spot—out of the wind," his father would say, and Hank would take the lead.

That's the way it would go for a while, the two of them stringing through pine and birch, zig-zagging to avoid the low spots. For a while Hank would almost forget his father was there. Then, suddenly he would jump at the sound of something crashing through the bushes. He'd turn around quickly and see his father holding a limb, smiling that mocking grin. Throwing chunks of wood to make a racket was his favorite forest trick.

He pulled his cap down over his eyes to keep out the heavy snow. He had looked around for red clothing before he left the house. Deer season. The lakeshore would be no place for browns, no place for anything but reds. He found a brand new jacket hanging from a hook at the entrance to the basement, a deer tag pinned to the back. Wim must have got a license somehow.

The lay of the woods came back to him as if it were only yesterday he had tramped through. An old cabin used to stand somewhere close, he remembered. Successive spring thaws had roiled the earth beneath and shifted the walls in such a way as to make you feel off balance when you stood inside. Once there was an old mattress there, its stuffings strewn by shotgun blasts. He tried to locate the spot where the cabin stood.

There was only the sound of his feet and the low bay of the surf on the lakeshore half a mile or less to the east.

"So it's another season without that buck."

"Dad?" he said. "Where are you?"

"Here," he said, his voice hushed. "Over here."

Wim Pietenpol sat beneath an upturned stump, fifteen yards ahead, his rifle crossed over his lap. He wore the same red plaid jacket he always wore. He spoke very quietly. "At least you dressed the right color. Where is your gun?"

"I thought I'd let you get the buck, Dad."

"Now no venison for sure this winter." He motioned Hank over to a stump, three or four yards from his post, to his left. "This spot is what I picked out for you. Come on now, sit down here then if you won't hunt. There's no deer through here yet. You probably chased them all off to the next county."

"I'm sorry, Dad."

"Ach, sorry. For years I haven't shot that buck. You

think maybe I will be angry if it takes one more?" He pointed again. "Here," he said. "Scrape off the snow or your pants will get wet."

"You couldn't shoot a deer and you know it, Dad," Hank said.

"So now my son says I'm not man enough—is that it?" He raised his rifle. "I tell you what. I know it is hard for a preacher to keep his mouth closed once, but you sit here with me and you will see what I can shoot."

The grays of the forest emerged from a slowly brightening sky. The snow fell perfectly, crowning Wim's cap in chalky clumps and fleecing his shoulders.

"When I saw you come, I thought maybe some idiot would shoot you here in the dark. That's what I was thinking." His lips barely moved when he spoke. "This woods is full of idiot hunters from the city nowadays. It's not like it was once."

Hank pulled up his collar.

His father's voice was deliberately hushed. "It would be something, a little one and a wife left behind, a good wife."

Even in winter it was the birches that were most beautiful. In the old days they would strip bark from felled birch, peel it off in soft, thin sheets, like paper.

"You think of it sometime. Bang!—your life is gone. What then?"

"Dad," Hank said, "the deer." He raised a finger to his lips. He watched his father's eyes wander across the trail, blinking—once, twice—methodically owl-like.

"So what is it?—I can't tell my own son something important—just because of a deer?"

To hear his father whisper was worth the trip to the woods, Hank thought.

"Not now, Dad," he said.

Long strips of snow fell noiselessly from birch branches and spotted the woods' rug, already beginning to glow in the advance of daylight.

"Those deer don't know either that the end is near.

They come here through the trees. It is any other morning to them, and then bang!—and that's it." Wim took his hand from the trigger and sliced through the air, palm down.

"Why do you think you always have to teach me things, Dad? I'm a grown man now, for pity's sake."

Wim's hand settled back on the rifle. Steam pumped from his nose in long funneled clouds. "So now you're thirty and you think everything there is to know is already up there in your head?"

Hank bent over slowly. "My goodness—I'm a missionary—"

"Ja, and your father is a retired machinist—so what? You think maybe that being a missionary buys you grace?"

"It's not grace that I'm talking about, Dad. It's the way you act towards me, as if I'm a boy—always homilies, those little moral lessons. You're job is over now, Dad."

"You think so?" Wim held his finger in the air. "Corrie and me, we know already it is your own life—you and Ila and now Tony too. Maybe that's why I can't stop." His hand flexed, released, then flexed again around the barrel. "Maybe it was easier for Corrie and me when you slept alone in your room." All the time he nodded, as if agreeing with himself. "Now you don't want a father."

"I'm not asking you to stop being my father, Dad. I just wish you wouldn't insist on trying to wrestle me all the time." He watched his father in silhouette. "I'm not saying you can't—"

"So tell me, Hank—you like this liberation theology, don't you?"

It was the woods that made Wim mute his tone, and his hushed voice, Hank thought, softened his words. He didn't want this one again; he was tired of it already, even though it had been only a few days.

"You just can't turn your back on the lives of poor people. So you preach Christ, but you don't lift a hand against oppression—then what have you done?"

"Ach, oppression. You tell me once what is oppression—" Wim lifted the single-shot from his knees and stood it against the roots of the upturned stump behind him. He turned toward Hank. "So you work on those people's lives—and you change the government too. You get rid of the Fascist dictator—then what? Maybe you bury the people in a fancier casket, that's what you do—" He pushed his thumb into his chest. "Here you change them, and then you got change. Otherwise, what have you done?"

Hank waited for the constant wash of the lakeshore to fill the emptiness left behind his father's words.

"Am I right?" Wim said.

He chose silence because he had never beaten his father with words. The lakeshore had attracted him this morning, not another argument and another sermon. He looked through the trees as if he were sitting here alone, waiting for the big buck.

"We got to get things straight, Hank. I have to know where my own son stands—"

Silence had its own inherent nobility, its own kind of passive righteousness—even its own blessed tradition.

"You cannot join with Communists, Hank. You cannot do that." He slapped his knee with the back of his hand. "Ach, why do I waste my breath when my son won't talk to me?" He leaned back, his hands on his knees.

"Because you don't want to talk, Dad—you only want to preach. That's all. You only want to preach."

For a time, his father's nodding seemed the only movement in the forest.

Wim stood and shoved his hands in his pockets, thumbs out. "By now Corrie is up. She will make some breakfast, and talk."

Hank watched him step away slowly and quietly, his rifle still leaning up against the stump where he had left it.

"Dad—" Hank said, but his father shoved his attention away with a mittened hand and walked away slowly through the trees, the red plaid of his old jacket turning darker with each step.

Hank moved to his father's place and retrieved the rifle, brushing the snow from the butt with his glove. Without thinking he laid it over his knees and put his finger on the trigger watching the old man's clean movements through the woods. Wim wasn't so agile as he once was; his darkened figure shifted in and out of the broken pattern of trees in the distance, visible only in contrast with the backdrop of snow. The higher branches cut through the gray early morning overcast. Now and then a twig snapped under Wim's boots.

Hank jerked his glove off with his teeth and touched the cold barrel, leaving prints on the steel.

Hundreds of times he had tailed that plaid jacket through these woods. He watched it slip into the distance now, into the shallow darkness, until his father's presence was visible only by the slightest movement. Then he was gone. Hank knew his father expected that he would be following, that he would be behind him when he got to the car. Like he always had done, always following. Maybe if he looked back and didn't see his son behind him—maybe if he didn't follow him right away.

He was alone in the woods, sitting on a stump with his fingers on cold steel, his father's single-shot. He strained to hear even a whisper of his father's movements. He wanted to hear him, because it was strange to be alone now.

The crack of a rifle skipped off the trees and snarled through the vacant stillness.

Probably his father had been right about the deer. It might have been just a matter of minutes before they came through his stand. He'd seen little groups of deer so often before in these woods, a few does first, then the buck following, slowly, ears up, head up, somehow sensing alien presence. When he was a boy, his father would look at him and nod, to be sure his son would see them, maybe four or five tan bodies on stick-like legs. And then he'd make a noise, and all of them would glide off, as if the earth were hard rubber, their white tails flaring through the trees.

He heard no second shot.

He listened for the hunter, for any noise of movement through the woods—a yell, even the sound of a wounded buck kicking up the leaves or crashing through the sticks and saplings poking out of the snows like cut wires. But only the echo of the shot was there, whining in his ears.

It had to be a good shot then, a perfect shot; there would be no chase, no long trek through the snow, no path of blood.

He turned toward the road, thinking maybe he could catch some motion in the trees. The shot had seemed so close. He told himself it must have been close to his father.

Or it may have been his father. The idea seemed so impossible that he smiled at having imagined it—his own father, a man who loved these woods, lying here in the perfect November snow, shot dead. His own father, dead. It was an odd thought, he told himself.

It was nearly daylight, but the snowy sky kept a pall of gray through the woods, the kind of semi-darkness that robbed the pines of their green tones and left them cloaked in black. Wim's plaid coat didn't shine its red in this kind of darkness. He had watched his father walk away, and he had seen no red. Only his movement made him distinguishable.

Hank looked again into the trees, thinking that some odd image might shake loose between the straight black trunks rising from the new snow. There was nothing.

It was foolish to think his father was shot, he told himself. Wim Pietenpol spent too many years here in these woods, too many Sunday afternoons, too many dawns, to die here.

No movement, no bounding deer, no shouting.

He looked around, his eyes stopping where any cluttered angle seemed out of place, where a clump of dirt rose like a blot from the snow, where any form or shape looked even vaguely exotic, as if it didn't belong to the contour of the woods. He flipped the rifle under his arm and stood, as if standing would allow him to see farther. Still there was no sign of movement.

Of course there were more hunters today than in the old days. His father had even said so, more hunters from the city—idiot hunters, his father had called them. Some idiot hunter could have mistaken his father's movements. Some trigger-happy hunter from the city.

He wanted to yell, but there was something that told him it was only his fear pursuing him, that said yelling out for his father through the trees would make him seem odd, even crazy. He sat again where his father had sat and tried to calm himself. Told himself it was ridiculous and even childish to think the worst, to jump to horrible conclusions. Paranoid.

He felt the very real loss of his father in his stomach. It was as if life itself had been pulled from beneath him, and he had been left fatherless, suspended in a world he neither knew nor trusted. It stayed there with him, right beneath his ribs like some widening crevice that threatened more of him. What would it be like without him? Miles, thousands of miles, even cultures away, he had lived with his wife and his own son. For years he had been away from his father, far away. But it was that crimson image in the snow that ate away at his stomach and grew like some ravaging virus into his emotions.

He felt unable to stop himself from crying. Suspended—he felt suspended, hanging from some thread over a colorless world that no longer looked at all familiar. His father was dead now, gone. For years he hadn't needed his father, and now, when Wim Pietenpol was gone he felt callously abandoned, even angry at being left in this damned world without him.

He stood again and looked through the trees. Still no movement anywhere. Someone should have yelled if a deer was shot. If they didn't kill it, the deer would have run—there would have been some noise, rampage, a wounded deer, an anxious hunter pushing through the snow. But there was no sound.

He started walking, tracing the steps his father had left, the waffle prints. Already he could see him there, lying in the snow, face down, no one around, some blasted city hunter long ago run off when he'd seen what he'd done. There would be tracks there at his father's body, then long steps away through the snow.

He started to run, the rifle in his hands.

It wasn't right of him to die that way. He hadn't given his son a chance to tell him the truth—how much he needed him, how the world would be so much bigger without him, so much more unknown. He hadn't told his father those things.

"Dad," he yelled.

His father was dead. He had no home anymore. What was there to come back to now, without his father? The woods turned foreign around him, some other country. Without his father, this wasn't the woods he had walked in as a child.

He ran faster. "Dad!" he yelled again. The sound of his voice rang through the trees.

Everything seemed unfamiliar now. What would he say to his mother? She hated guns. Her house wouldn't be the same without his father. The dining room would be different if his dad wasn't in his chair at the head of the table. And the bedroom. His father wouldn't be there across the wall, and his voice wouldn't be there. It was as if he were suspended, left hanging with nowhere to touch down, unable to reach the ground, to feel the earth beneath his feet.

"Dad, where are you?" He tripped on a root and sprawled in the snow, still clinging to the single-shot, but

he scrambled quickly to his feet and kept running between the trees, heavy rims of snow clinging around his
wrists to the linings of his gloves.

Even Ila would be different without him, the business
of fatherhood so much worse, harder, mysterious. It was
as if his father had left him at the controls of some huge
machine he didn't fully understand how to operate. Anger. It was anger he felt, his father simply abandoning
him here, alone in the cold of this strange woods.

"Dad!" he yelled again. "Where are you?" He neglect-
ed the path when his eye caught some movement between the trees. "Dad?" he said.

He found them standing in a circle of pines, three men
looking down at the lifeless body of a heavy buck, their
rifles still in their hands.

When he stopped running, he leaned over, hands on
his knees, and tried to regain his wind. It was the buck.
The buck was dead.

Short, heavy spurts of breath steamed up from its
lungs.

The men didn't notice him standing there. One of
them drew a long knife from his belt and stooped over
the carcass. He poked the glimmering steel into the belly
and sliced through the hide, pulling the blade toward
him in an even motion, slowly, smoothly. Steam gushed
from the opening, and the bluish entrails slid out in a
film of red.

"Can you believe this guy was all alone—this big
guy—not even a doe out in front," the man said. "Come
right here out of the pines, all by his lonesome." The
man laughed as if it were a wonderful joke.

"He just come right out of those pines—just out of
nowhere, really," the man said, looking up at the others
while his hand reached up into the buck's empty carcass.

"You see an old man walk by here?" Hank said. "Old
man with a plaid coat?"

The man reached up to push his glasses up his nose.

"Could have shot that bastard," he said. "What business an old unarmed man got out here when it's the first day of deer season?" He didn't wait for an answer.

Hank took off his glove to slap away the snow, and steam rose from his fingers. It was Abraham he thought of—and a ram mysteriously drawn from a thicket. It's what his father would have said himself.

Dawn had come. Misty light spread through the trees from a hidden sun somewhere behind the swirl of thick clouds that were themselves unseen through the gauze of lake snow.

He left the hunters slowly, unnoticed, and cradled the single-shot in his arms, following the waffle prints, until he came to the road, where he stood alone in the snow.

Even the pavement was masked in white now, Wim's own footprints deep and black and soggy.

Hank's car stood facing east with another and the truck further down the road toward the shoreline. But his father's car was already gone, its presence recorded only in the Y-shaped series of lines where Wim had turned it around west, toward the town, toward home.

All the way up the hill above the woods, two perfectly straight tire tracks cut dark parallel lines into the chalky whiteness. As far as he could see, his father's path was still out there before him, until finally it disappeared in the husky incandescence of heavy lake snow.

T H R E E

T he damp lake cold had pinned itself to his cheeks, as if it were a mask. The kitchen heat warmed his chest first, his insides, then stretched up through his shoulders and down his arms and legs and slowly reached up to his face, as if home and the kitchen table and a steaming triangle of coffee cups transmitted warmth themselves, which pleased him.

"And you didn't know the men?" his father asked, his elbows squared up over the table.

"I'm sure they weren't from town," Hank said.

Despite the familiar sameness of the kitchen—the formica table in the corner, its leaves turned down, the intermittent growling of the Frigidaire, the sharp edge of brewed coffee—Hank urged change on the place, as if what had happened in the woods should cause some odd twist in his vision.

"It's not the same anymore," Wim said. "Now they come from the city to hunt here in these woods—men with fancy rifles. I wish they'd stay home."

Hank struggled to find the words to tell him what had happened, what he had felt for those few minutes alone. He didn't know how to say it—whether to make it sound like a joke or something serious.

"The pick-up had a bumper sticker—'I'd rather be dancing,' it said." Hank folded one leg over the other and sat back from the table, his jacket hanging from the chair.

"That buck is on his way to the city now," Wim said. "It makes me angry."

Early, Corrie always brewed a full pot of coffee, took a cup or two herself, them emptied the rest into a tall, white vacuum bottle that she stood up on the counter next to the toaster for the rest of the morning. They were sitting there already when he got home, drinking from the old cups, off-white, insides laced with thin brown cracks. Corrie sat with her hands around her own, as if it were she who had been to the woods.

"So the big buck is dead, Corrie," Wim said, "shot dead by some stranger in those woods. Almost like stealing."

"You know already what I think anyway," she said.

Wim twisted his lips as if he had just taken a good punch.

Hank liked seeing his father scolded in Corrie's quiet way, the way only she could reprimand him, eyes down as if it weren't right for a wife to be telling her husband he was wrong.

"Remember this, too, Hank," he said. "Don't ever look for sympathy from a woman. They give it all to their boys, and when the boys are grown, the well is dry. You'll see that, too. Just watch—"

Hank reached up to open the top button of his shirt. "Dad," he said, "there's more to it. There's something else. The funniest thing happened—"

He didn't want to say "funny" really, because it wasn't funny.

"I was sitting there when you left and I heard the shot, see?—and there was only one. I started to think about it—you know, about the idiot hunters and everything, and I got to thinking that it could have been you—" He waited momentarily, looking down at the edge of the table and pinching the top between his fingers.

"Every time he goes out with a gun that's what I see in my mind," Corrie said. "For these many years already."

"Then what?" Wim said.

"What do you mean?" Hank said.

"I mean, then what?—so what did you do?"

He wanted it to be a clean profession, a statement of belief in his own father, but Wim had a way of jerking things around his way, so that it became confession instead. He was nervous now. "I took off after you, running," he said. "That's when I found the men with the deer."

"The Lord was with you," Wim said, sipping his coffee.

"What on earth does that mean?"

Wim pulled his elbows back and dropped his hands to the arms of the captain's chair. "You're the one who could have been shot, running through the woods like that with all those city boys around."

"You aren't listening to me, Dad." Wim seemed so terribly unmoved. "It was a horrible feeling—to think that you were gone—"

Corrie rose from the table and retrieved the vacuum bottle.

"What do you think, Corrie? This boy of ours is finally grown up. Now he knows that he still needs his father."

She poured coffee into each of their cups, sealed up the bottle, and sat again. Wim sat there nodding and smiling, itching his arm through the wool shirt.

"It's not a joke," Hank said. "I wasn't laughing when it happened. It was this awful sinking feeling as if you'd left me alone—" He looked at his mother for understanding. "I can't really describe it—"

His own inability to say it all left the whole room in silence. He picked up the cup quickly and blew lightly over the coffee. Corrie's little radio stood in the corner by the sink, the volume up just high enough for them to hear a someone forecasting the weather.

Hank looked at his father, but Wim's eyes seemed unsettled, even distracted. He wished he could take his father's shoulders and pin them to the wall, shout at him, tell him clearly how much he had missed him for those few minutes. But Wim's face was blank, stone-like.

"Do you hear what I'm saying, Dad?" he said.

"Some things are running down now, but I still got my ears," he said, but he never looked at Hank, and the only sense that Hank could get of his being affected in any way was the fact that he seemed almost speechless.

"I missed you," Hank said. "I never realized that before."

Wim rolled his tongue around in his closed mouth and looked at Corrie. "Yup," he said, nodding.

Hank wanted it to be so good, wanted his father to understand and appreciate what he'd felt, what he'd been through.

"Well, I got to put that rifle away," Wim said. "I got the case in my car." He pushed himself back from the table and stood. "You could have been arrested for taking that rifle back with no case—" He picked up his cup and left them there, heading for the hall and the basement stairs.

Hank and Corrie listened until the back door slapped shut behind him. Then she laughed. "He can be sometimes such a strange one—your father." She shook her head.

"Why can't I talk to him? Why can't I tell him what I really felt, Mother? I don't understand—"

She pulled herself close to the table and reached for Hank's arm. "He won't let you," she said. "He knows what he wants from his own son, and that's all—"

"Why? Sometimes I don't understand why he's constantly after me the way he is. It's all so formal with him. Sometimes I feel like his apprentice or something—just a kid learning some trade—"

Wim came back in from outside, carrying the rifle. From the kitchen table, they could just see his head and shoulders and the barrel. He didn't bother to look their way.

"That man loves you more than anything in this world," she said. "I remember once—way back when you were just a baby. And Wim says to me then—it was one night in that first winter, and already you were asleep. He would read his Bible at night, before bed. He doesn't do that anymore. I don't know why. Together we read in the mornings. But that one night he says to me that maybe he is guilty of idolatry." She couldn't help but laugh, remembering.

" 'Idolatry,' I say to him, 'My husband?' "

" 'Maybe I love that boy more even than the Lord,' he says to me."

"Even then I laughed at him—not out loud, of course, but in here." She pointed to her chest, and bowed her head, as if she were explaining some weakness that a son should never see.

"You wait," she said, "a couple minutes and cigar smoke from down there." Behind glasses that had grown thicker through the years, her almost colorless eyes sparkled, and she tightened her lips straight across her face as if she were trying to look slightly perturbed.

"How do you live with him?—"

"What a question to ask. He's not my father. He's my husband."

The screech of his stool across the basement floor stretched up the stairs and into the kitchen.

"There is no stronger man that I know in the world," she said, "but sometimes even strength can be weakness, I know."

His mother's hair was always dry and very curly, growing out in a broad circle around her face, like hemp bleached perfectly white. Her straight teeth protruded just slightly from her smile. Hank thought she had always had wrinkles, but he noticed them now, the way they ran in semi-circles down the front of her neck, like thin necklaces, one atop the other.

"That's a warm housecoat, I bet," he said.

"It was a present, from your father, years ago," she told him. She ran her fingers beneath the collars to pull it up tighter around her neck.

"I bought one like that for Ila when I was in seminary—she picked it out, of course."

Corrie pulled at the corduroy with both hands. "This one was Wim's gift—one Saturday afternoon maybe ten years ago." She looked down at her elbows and rubbed the spots where the fabric was worn. "For no reason he gave it to me—your father did."

Hank had not sat here often with them, and he recognized what he felt now as guilt over memories of what might have been. He wondered why it was he never returned from college, whether it was some unconscious hatred of his father or simply the love of freedom he felt when miles separated them. For years he thought his desire to stay away from home was merely a recognition that the city had more to offer him than Easton did— once he had left it. He didn't think he had consciously avoided his father; he had never hated him really. He wasn't able to hate his father, because hate was an emotion unavailable to him in a moral world where, by commandment, even one's enemies were to be loved.

But he felt now, at this very moment, what his staying away must have done to them—their only son, a boy of nineteen already committed to the ministry, whose summers away from home had almost snubbed them, at least in the eyes of the village.

"Maybe this is something I missed," Hank said, "you know, sitting here with you over coffee and talking like real people. I mean, I never sat here that often with you. We never talked—"

"Always you were off to school, Hank," she said. She laid a plate of cinnamon rolls in front of him.

In the silence between them, both of them listened to the sounds of the house beginning to come alive. It was after seven already, and from the upstairs came movements between the three bedrooms. Ila was awake. Downstairs, they could hear Wim zipping up the rifle case, then opening and closing the door of the cabinet where all his guns were stored.

"I want us to have a nice time together, Mom," he said. "I really do."

"So does he—I know he does," she said.

Wim made his way back upstairs slowly, then stopped to hang the insulated vest he was wearing over a hook in the hall.

One time Hank had seen him break, just one time, years ago, when Hank was just a boy. He and some friends had been caught stealing from fishing lines—

little spools of transparent filament—from the hardware store. Hank had gone to bed early that night, because he knew that his father would find out later.

Wim walked into the kitchen with one of his carved birds in his hand. "This is for Ila—I don't want to forget," he said, standing it up on the counter near the phone.

Hank would always remember that night. From his bedroom, he heard the bell at the back door. He had crept out of bed and hunched over at the screen on the window above the porch. The two men's voices spoke in tones so low that from upstairs the conversation seemed barely more than a whisper.

Ten minutes later, back in bed, feigning sleep, he listened to his father's every step up the stairs. Wim sat at the foot of his bed and spoke as if his son were very much awake. There was no denying anything, Hank knew. It was something they did for thrills, for the excitement of getting away with it.

But his father's sobbing shook the bed. He sat there in the darkness with his head in his hands. Hank had been in sixth grade, he remembered, because it was the same year the little league won the county championship without him. But it was the only time he had ever seen his father weak.

"When does that little guy wake up?" Wim said.

It took months after that for things to be the same again. Hank remembered painting the fence out back, a white lattice fence, a job he otherwise would have hated; but he remembered wishing that he could paint forever, stay out of his father's way, keep himself busy with something, prove himself somehow, bring himself back into saintliness with all the white paint.

"Back home he's got us both up by this time," Hank said. "Seems like you two really tucker him out."

That night years ago his father's weeping was his only sermon.

Ila came down the steps, Tony over her shoulder, peeking out fearfully, his thumb in his mouth. "So, the great white hunters are back already," she said.

"How we going to get all the frozen venison back to San Salvador, Ila? You got any ideas—"

"You didn't get one—"

"We got six," Hank said.

"You're kidding—"

Corrie reached for Tony, but the boy turned away. His hair reached up straight in the back as if it had been brushed.

"This man of yours had a chance at the biggest buck in the woods, and he let it go," Wim said.

"Good for you," Ila said.

Hank pulled out the fourth chair for his wife.

"So what really happened?" she said. Tony clung to his mother's shoulders, as if he'd forgotten his grandparents completely overnight.

"This husband of yours goes charging through the woods like a bull when he thinks his own father is dead—that's the story," Wim said. He tried to make a joke of it.

"Dad—" Hank said.

"No, no, you can't deny it, Hank. You did it too, you know. You told me so."

They all looked at him, all three of them, Corrie finally rising and taking the boy from his mother, then holding him tightly against her shoulder and patting his back.

"I don't get it," Ila said. "What happened?"

Wim filled his mouth with cinnamon roll.

Hank shrugged his shoulders. "I heard this shot, see. Dad wasn't around, and I started thinking that the one shot I heard was in him—in Dad." The strangeness of it—how it sounded even when he explained it—the oddness pinched him, embarrassed him. "It's not so weird really—quite often it takes more than one shot to get a big buck." He looked at his father.

"Tell Ila what you were thinking, Hank," his father said. "Go on and tell her—"

"It wasn't so dumb. I had walked right through that place not a half hour before, and I didn't see a soul. So what was I to think?"

Wim chomped on the roll and kept nodding, urging him on with a smile.

"Besides, that jacket of yours isn't really red at all anymore."

Ila took a swallow of coffee from Hank's cup. "So what's the big joke here?" she said.

"I can't help but laugh to think of him—boom, boom, boom—like a bull through the trees. Hah! You think of it once. It's a wonder them hunters didn't shoot Hank dead right there, maybe even out of fear—"

"I was scared," Hank said.

Ila said she still didn't get it, but Hank felt no obligation to explain what he thought should be obvious. He had already told his father, confessed it, pure and simple. She laid her arm over his shoulder and tugged at him for an answer. "Henry," she said.

"It was scary to have to think of a world without Dad," he said. "That's what I was thinking."

Corrie asked Ila if she wanted her own cup.

"And for all those years I thought this one here was a mama's boy," Wim said.

"Let's just forget it," Hank said. "You want me to apologize or what?"

Wim smiled. "So tell me, Ila, when was it that Hank lost his sense of humor?"

She stood up and walked over to the cupboard. "He never had a sense of humor. You never let him laugh." She pulled a cup out, walked back to her husband, and took the white thermos from in front of her father-in-law.

Hank told her that that wasn't true. Quietly, he told her, and he could feel her turn stone cold next to him.

"Cheeerie," Tony said.

"Tony wants breakfast," Hank said. He wrapped his arm around Ila.

Ila said she would get him a bowl.

"She's just trying to tell you that it wasn't funny, Dad—the whole business of me thinking you were dead, it wasn't funny. Not at all. Not to me."

"I can't help but laugh to think of you running between the trees—like a bull—bang! bang! bang!—"

"I felt like you deserted me." He tried to laugh to make it sound overstated. "That's the way I felt—like you left me all alone on the face of the earth." He spoke directly to him now, even though it was difficult to look into his face. "You can laugh, but for a while I was angry that you were dead."

The four of them sipped at the same time.

"Cheeerie," Tony said.

Wim's silence sank into a stare. "Corrie, you know how good a cigar would be right now?" he said.

Corrie fed Tony his Cheerios.

"I just want you to know that it wasn't funny, Dad. Not at all. The way it all happened was strange, but it wasn't funny." He pulled lightly at the housecoat over Ila's shoulders.

The radio voice listed births at three local hospitals, a string of Dutch names.

With Wim, conversation rarely tip-toed, but when it did, when pace dragged on an uphill subject, the silence of his default was itself provoking. Hank had felt it before, and it bothered him. Silence made the peace even more uneasy. Besides, Hank thought, it was so foolishly childish. The old man's obstinate quiet was his way of pleading for something more than consolation and slightly less than absolution. He wanted some kind of apology before he'd play along again, something fabricated, some deference that would play like homage to his age or wisdom, or his exalted image of the office of father. Until he got it, he'd close down the subject, whatever it was they were in.

So Hank said he was sorry, even though he didn't know why he should be, even though he knew he was saying it merely because it was expected of him.

Wim palmed the top of the empty cup and turned the bottom in a circle over the formica. He pointed at Corrie with one raised finger. "You see that now, Hank. You see how your mother picked up the spoon to feed the boy. You watch her now, because that is how all men go bad." He picked the cup off the table and softly hammered it into his hand. "You see how she does that? They're all alike, those women. I've seen it. You should have seen that woman there hang on you when you was a boy. Of course, Henry Pietenpol was a miracle, but already we told you that."

He sat back easily now, the empty cup held in both hands.

"Corrie and me used to joke about Abraham and Sarah and how they laughed when the Lord said, 'Go ahead now—finally it is the right time.' 'Sure,' they told him, 'sure, you bet we can, and us so old too.'" He pulled the back of his arm along his face, wiping his mouth with the sleeve.

Corrie spoonfed Tony.

"Soon enough that boy will feed himself, Corrie," Wim said.

Corrie didn't look up. "Then he will be just so smart as his grandfather," she said.

"This is what I'm telling you, Hank. Even your own Ila. She is a woman of today, I guess, but even Ila will spoil that boy, mother him until he can't get along without her—you see once." Wim reached for the thermos. "And then one day when he has to look himself for a wife, he will look for one who will mother him. This is the truth." He splashed hot coffee in his cup and took a sip, never dropping his grin. "So someday Tony gets his own wife and he still wants to be mothered, and his wife will say—she'll even get angry with him—'I'm not your mother, see?' That's what she'll tell him." He flexed his shoulders, laughing broadly. " 'I'm not your mother,' she will say, but that woman will bring up her own boy just like they all do, feeding him his Cheerios." He turned to Ila. "There's the problem all men face." He said it as if it really should have been written somewhere in the Scriptures.

Hank guessed that Ila was too angry to speak.

"And that's the way it is with every generation. And that's why we have this trouble, Hank—us men with women. You see what—"

"That's nonsense," Ila said. "What on earth does that have to do with you and Hank?" She leaned her shoulders in toward the table as if to throw off Hank's hand.

Wim mouthed the rest of a cinnamon roll and smiled. Whatever it was that had been said wasn't meant for him anyway. He tipped his eyebrows when he ate, as if eating was taking all of his attention. He turned his face mute.

"This Tony is a hungry boy," Corrie said. Milk ringed his little mouth and narrowed to a white point on his chin.

"Somehow it is Corrie's fault that you two don't get along—is that it?"

"Ila—" Hank said.

"I won't stand for it," she said. "I won't let him pass his own blasted problems off on his wife. He's just avoiding the whole thing."

"Ila doesn't—"

"Don't apologize for me. I've watched you sit for two weeks worrying about how things are going to go between you and your father. Now don't pretend this whole problem doesn't exist. What's the matter with you?" She pushed herself away from him and stared blindly out in front at her cup, fear and anger fusing in her eyes.

"Ila—"

She left the room crying.

"Mama," Tony said. "Mama."

Corrie told the boy to eat his Cheerios.

The radio played "I Will Sing of My Redeemer," sung by a male quartet with a heavy bass. Then came a man selling used cars.

"Look, I'm sorry about what Ila said," Hank told them. "She's upset about some things. I think it's just coming back to this country again. It's kind of a shock—"

"You tell me what she means—" Wim said. The question was printed in the lines of his father's face.

Just for a moment he tried to concentrate on the interior of his church in San Salvador, the chairs, the pulpit, the rack full of pamphlets and tracts in the back of the sanctuary. He tried to see the whole place full on a Sunday morning.

"I don't understand," Wim said.

Hank folded his hands in front of him. "She doesn't understand how we are, you know—you and me. She thinks that we don't understand each other. She thinks we fight because we don't get along." His eyes cut a straight line back and forth between mother and father. "She doesn't understand." He tried to find some way to get through to him. "Ach, you know how women are, Dad—they can't fight and stay friends. Not like men."

"You think maybe she doesn't like me?"

"She doesn't understand you. We aren't like her family, you and I. Of course she likes you—you know, the way you two kid around together—"

"I think maybe she needs you now," Corrie said. "You better see once how she is."

Ila was sitting on the bed, but she wasn't crying now; her anger had overtaken that. She wouldn't look at Hank.

"It's all right, honey," he said.

"Don't baby me, Hank, and don't tell me that everything is okay." Hank felt her hazy cold. "Maybe it's not my business at all—the way you and your father get along, but it can't go on like this. It's wrong. Don't you see that?" The chill was gone the minute she looked at him. "My goodness, you're a preacher—It's not right for a man and his son—"

"You don't understand, Ila. It's always been this way. It's different than you're used to. He doesn't know another way to be a father."

"That doesn't make it right."

"They're not your parents, Ila. So every week we get this little tape from your folks, a little Sunday dinner chatter—who's getting who something for whose birthday and what grade your baby sister's getting for reciting Bible verses—those cute little tapes. My folks just aren't like that. You've got to take my father for what he is—"

"You can't do that yourself. Don't tell me how to take him when you can't. You sweated this coming home more than anything else on the furlough, didn't you? I could see it in you already before we left. You don't say it—maybe you don't even recognize it, but is this the way it's supposed to be, this everlasting tension?"

"Maybe it's in you, Ila."

"What do you mean? You call this a homecoming? This whole house is strung on high wires. You won't even admit it."

"I don't know—"

" 'I don't know?' Don't say it like that—'I don't know.' " She pulled away from him and stood. "You sound like your own father. That's the scary part, Hank." She walked away from him and stood at the open door of the closet. "Your father's clothes in here—" she said. She pulled a sleeve up to her face. "Sometimes I get scared that it's going to be the same way with you and Tony—you know? I mean that you're going to be to Tony—"

"Ila, you're being silly—"

"Why is that silly? You say your father knows only one way of relating to his son—how many ways do you know?"

"You're wrong."

"Look at these. Here's some old suits. You can put these on and preach in church when we get back to El Salvador. Look just like him—"

"I don't like your sarcasm," Hank said.

"It scares me sometimes." She turned her back completely. "Don't avoid it. Let's make sense out of it this time. I don't want to leave here with this anxiety I've felt every time before. He treats you like a child—"

"He's always pushed me that way—"

"I know that," she said, coming back to the bed. "But why? What does he want you to be that you aren't?"

He spreads his hands around her waist. "It's just the way he is," he said.

"That's not true." Ila laid her arms over his shoulders. "It's only you he picks on. It's not Tony or me or his own wife. It's just you. Can't he treat you like a human being? Why?—"

Hank pulled her close to him. "When you live with it for so many years, you accept it—it's the way things are. I've never asked why, maybe because I thought he wouldn't let me. 'Now you listen to this, Hank'—'But here, now you remember this once too—' It's always been like that."

She rested her head on his chest. "This time make it change."

Hank felt her crying in her staggered breaths. He pulled her closer, then sat her down next to him. "Why does it feel like such a dirty conspiracy?" he said. "Why am I whispering to my own wife?"

"You want to know why?" She held him away. "Because he's never been human to you, and you can't even think of him as human. He's too big."

"He's only my father—"

"Then why do you always take his side? You apologized for me, didn't you?"

"It wasn't really an apology."

"You did, didn't you? You can't imagine him being

wrong, because he's your father and he's too stinking big in your mind to question."

He knew she was right. He had been embarrassed at the way she had behaved, and the things she had said to him. As if it were desecration to speak to him in those tones. "My father made me," he said.

Ila let his words stay there in front of him until they turned rotten in his ears.

"I've got to tell you what happened, Ila—I mean, in the woods. He didn't understand—maybe he can't, I don't know."

Ila put her hand on his leg and leaned away from him to pull a Kleenex from the box at the side of the bed.

"I thought he was dead. I could see him lying in the snow. The most vivid dream I ever had, seeing him there—"

Ila looked at him, in his eyes, the Kleenex wound in her fingers.

"It wasn't easy to face the world. That's what was scary. I mean, you can say what you want about how we get along, but he's there, you know. And he loves me. He never tells me that, but he doesn't have to. I know he does. And the thought of being without him just about leveled me." He laughed as it came out. "I mean I kept seeing myself falling into some deep well with no bottom."

"Hank, for seven years you've been thousands of miles away. You don't need—"

"It's not that I need him. I don't." He leaned his elbows on his knees. "It's just that someday I might, for whatever reason, and then maybe he won't be around."

"You told him?" She put her hand up on his shoulder.

"I told him, but he wasn't listening, or he couldn't, or I don't know— He didn't see it quite like I did."

"But nothing's changed—"

"Maybe I just found out it's going to be difficult to live without him."

She smiled when he looked at her. "Ten years ago, for a cup of coffee I could have told you that much."

"I wouldn't have believed it ten years ago, either," he said. "It's like he says, Ila. It's like shooting ducks on the lake. You judge distance by standards that you aren't even aware of—a tree, an old barn, those old suits in there. Ten years ago I didn't realize my father was some ghost standard in me. Take that standard away—it's scary as hell itself because you've got nothing then. Maybe now I know what he's given me—"

She drew in a deep breath and released it slowly. "So nothing is going to change, and every trip back here we're going to have to put up with his endless sermons and his lousy condescension. Is that it?" She pinched him at the base of the neck, twisted his face toward her. "Why do you take it? Just tell me why?"

He thought he had told her everything. She let him go slowly, then stood and walked to the door. "I'm in trouble out there, I suppose."

Hank shook his head. "They're both hanging on Tony. I don't think he knows what you were talking about. Mom knows. She's committed to the old way—it's her own husband, you know. Dad probably thinks it's your period."

"He would—"

"You've got nothing to be scared of—"

"Who's scared?" She opened the door and faced the hallway. "I'll scream it out. I'm serious, Hank. I don't want to come back here again the same way."

"Ila—"

"I've seen other fathers and sons. I don't want my boy raised by a father like yours." She stood with her hand on the knob. "Don't get me wrong. I don't hate your father. I'm tired of the way he beats on you, and I don't want him turning you into another one of him. My goodness, Hank, one in the family is already too many."

He felt her standing there at the edge of laughter.

"It's not funny," she said, hiding her smile against the door.

"You're the one who's laughing."

Deliberately, she avoided him.

"Come here," he said, slapping the bed.

She said no.

"You'd rather face them than me, wouldn't you?"

She walked out, then turned back in around the corner of the door. "You bet I would."

"Come here," he said.

"I've got to apologize to your parents now."

"Come on," he said. "I demand you come here and sit—must I quote Scripture?"

"I don't like that look, that kind of grin in your eyes. I know that look."

Hank leaned back on his elbows. "It's that house coat you're wearing. Is that new?"

"You know whose this is." She brought both hands up against the door post, as if to keep herself from falling. He always said that Ila laughed well.

"But tell me the truth—" she said, standing up straight, "you really think those dinner tapes from my folks are silly?"

"Come here," he said.

Before church already on Sunday morning Corrie had fixed some ham sandwiches and taken out the beans and a jello salad for a quick lunch after the service. By one they had to be off because it would take five hours, Wim said, for them to get up north to Waubedon, to the little church where Hank was scheduled to take the vespers service as a guest pastor.

"Not to worry now about the boy," Wim said. Tony sat on his arm, clinging to his grandfather's neck. "You hear me—not to worry about my Tony. Me and Corrie will handle him."

"Grandpa," Tony said.

"See there, he says it already. We'll have him saying by heart the 23rd Psalm when you get back."

Corrie pulled her dish towel up around the boy's ear. They stood there on the front porch, waving them off.

"You drive careful now, too, Hank. If it is too slippery, then you pull over and call that church. They can get something else yet for tonight. Those little churches got elders who can read sermons." He managed somehow to point, even though he was holding his grandson. "You listen to me, Hank, because up north sometimes they get snow before we do and more too."

Hank nodded. It was very warm outside.

"Ja, you listen. Don't you take no chances with this boy's mother. You hear me? You, I don't worry so much about, but that woman—"

Corrie tried to hush him somewhat. Hank knew she was saying how it wasn't right for him to be yelling so in front of the neighbors on the Sabbath.

The car doors slapped shut, but his father's mouth kept moving and his arm kept pointing, even though the words never made it into the car.

"I'm surprised at Tony," Ila said. "I really thought he'd be crying, but look at him hold on your father."

The car started easily.

"What's he saying?" she said.

Hank hunched his shoulders. "Roll down your window if you want to listen."

Ila turned it down slowly, and Wim's voice slipped back in. "It's something about the car," she said.

Hank stopped in the driveway, opened the door and leaned out. "What is it?"

"You watch the gas," Wim said. "You get out there somewhere in those woods up north and there's not so many people. It's backward up there. Don't get stranded alone." He held the boy with both hands and ran down the walk. "And remember to have them check the oil, too, sometimes," he said. "Ila, you have to remind him or he will forget sure. That son of mine don't know beans about engines." Tony was smiling, waving. "You remind him, Ila. You I can count on."

Ila nodded, turning up her window.

Corrie herself came running down from the front door and grabbed the boy from her husband, then held him close to her in both arms. "Wim—my word—" They could see her lips scold her husband for his recklessness.

The warmth of the blue sky and the thin touch of southern winds rolled back the day-old snow cover, and the melting snow darkened the brown rows of the plowed fields into black-ridged furrows. Water stood in puddles on the road or ran in icy frenzy through roadside ditches, picking up topsoil slowly until brown creeks fed the muddy rivers that wound through the shoreline pastures. The day was already out of season, a gift of grace perhaps, one last warm taste of autumn's best before December's cold winter grip.

"Backward," she said. "Did you hear him say that, Hank? He said, 'Don't get stuck out there, it's backward.' Did you hear that?"

"What he meant was that we don't want to get ourselves stranded. Sometimes there's a long distance between towns." Hank cranked open the window to get a smell of the moisture in the plowed fields. He thought it was almost like spring. And Ila's voice sounded rather disappointing.

"I know what he meant. My goodness, Hank. You don't get it yourself, do you?"

"Get what?"

He waited, then looked at her. He hated the way she sometimes did that, acted like some comedian suspending the punchline until the audience got hungry. "Ila," he said.

"You're going to be mad," she said. "I'd better not say it."

"Ila—"

"Don't be mad?"

"Ila, don't you ever—"

"Now I'm going to get myself in trouble with you, too." She folded her arms across her chest. She removed the seatbelt and twisted around in the seat to half-face him.

"I wouldn't dare get mad now. If I were, I'd be fulfilling your expectations." He looked over at her again. "So what's with you—so daring today, going without a seatbelt?"

"It seems different without Tony," she said.

"You were going to tell me something. My dad said not to get stranded out there—"

"—Because it's backward. Don't you understand? As if civilization itself stops right there at the Easton village limits."

It didn't strike him as such an odd thing to say, but he knew she was waiting for some reaction. "That's quite funny," he said, motionless.

"I'm sorry." She turned away.

"Big city girl," Hank said. "Big city girl."

On a Sunday afternoon in November Hank knew that rural Wisconsin would be locked up tight as an ice-jammed river. The state highways cut through the hills and woods, walked slowly over long stretches of marshland and a dozen or more rural hamlets where the only measure of life was a ring of cars parked around a roadhouse with a lit beer sign. State roads were as safe as freeways on Sunday, football afternoons.

"I still can't get over the way Tony didn't cry about us leaving," Ila said. She turned on the radio and zipped through snippets of rock music until she found something soft.

"You would have been much happier if he would have cried, wouldn't you?" he said.

"Come on, Hank—"

"Really, if he would have cried you would have been

much more pleased than embarrassed." He put both
hands on the wheel. "But you wouldn't admit that anyway, would you?"

"I'm just surprised, that's all."

Hank was happy about the soft cover of music. Something triggered a mood in him that was as difficult to
quiet as it was easy to feel. Maybe it was Ila's remark
about Easton. Sometimes her citified condescension angered him, because she had no sense of the comfort and
love of small town provinciality. Easton had no shopping
centers, no symphony, no night clubs; somehow life was
impossible in such a fortress of boredom. He was sure
her putdowns were done in the manner of all sarcasm,
simple attempts to elevate the status of the speaker. It
was born into her—this city girl.

"Well, I'm happy Tony didn't cry," he said.

Maybe it was the fact that he had to preach tonight,
and the sermon was an old stand-by he could pull out on
request and deliver blindfolded. He didn't know what it
was, this crankiness that he felt, but it seemed to hang
about Ila with a gray aura, an untouchable nature, as if
he felt nothing at all for her. She seemed more than a car
width away, her mind working in ways he didn't care to
know. He wanted some cheap excuse to haul out all the
most elemental arguments in their marriage, line them
up one at a time on the dashboard, and start reading
them off like some multi-count indictment.

"How far is it?" she said.

He raised his left knee and sat back in the seat. "You
sick of it already?"

She turned toward him quickly, as if he had said something offensive. "I just wondered how far it was."

"We've only been gone an hour."

"Maybe you'd be happier if I crawled in the backseat
and slept—or the trunk." She faced him, and he didn't
like the feel of her eyes on him, not when he couldn't
stare back. "You got it again, don't you?" she said. "You

got that terrible moody sickness—it's there every time we leave your father."

He turned up the radio. "If I need an analyst, I'll pay for one," he said.

"I don't care what you think. It's that stinking sourness, that blasted pride—that's what always gets into you when we leave. Always. Because you can't leave him back there, that's why." She waited for him to bite back; he knew she was trying to draw him back into a fight. "You know it too, don't you? You start acting like him almost, maybe worse, because—"

She waited again, watching him.

"Say something, Hank."

The music's gentleness seemed oddly right at the moment.

She grabbed his arm and squeezed it with her fingers. "You're so sure there's nothing strange about you and your father, aren't you? You're so sure. 'You don't understand him, Ila,' you say. Maybe I don't. Maybe all that lecturing is what fathering is. But I won't have my son bullied." She pulled herself close to him, as if she were going to whisper. "And I won't have you acting like this—not to him, because he's your son. I'm your wife and I have to take it, but Tony's your own son. I don't want an Absalom, Hank."

Slowly her grip relaxed, and she moved back across the seat. She straightened her blouse behind her and twisted her legs around toward the front.

"It's some kind of mood come over me, Ila," he said. "I don't know what it is." He dropped his hands down and held the wheel at the bottom, resting his arms in his lap. "I'm sorry," he said.

F O U R

By Tuesday the furlough tour had taken them west as well as north. Beyond the Mississippi, the glacial hills bottomed into miles of flatland, and the rolling acres of trees thinned into spotty patches of elms or clumps of mammoth cottonwoods towering over barns and feed lots, in protection against stinging prairie winds. Seen from a distance, the farm groves grew like fur stoles around the buildings, their branches leafless in December, like so much dead brush. The wide yawn of turned-up land stretched out into a colorless early winter horizon, interrupted at half miles by homesteads—red or gray barns, a white frame house of several floors, two or three farm coops in odd dimensions, and around it all, the skirt of elms or poplar or cottonwoods.

The tour itself was a necessary evil, Hank thought. The churches had structured his travel, sent him across the upper plains, following a mapped string of colored pins, each of them some Dutch Reformed church hidden on the flatland. It was a necessary part of furlough, of course—keeping in touch—and it accomplished rather distasteful, but essential, public relations. He knew the churches saw the tour in much the same way he did. And sometimes the bloodless formality of obligation appeared obvious in the manner by which people greeted them. Hank and Ila Pietenpol were the church's missionaries to El Salvador after all, and their mission portrait, a handsome black and white pose showing Ila with her arms full of new baby, was pinned to a bulletin board somewhere in every church. It was only right that each pastor do his best to create some audience for them, no matter what the people themselves might have thought about having to come out to the church an extra night during the week.

By Wednesday, after one sermon, a soup supper slide presentation and an afternoon coffee luncheon with widows, Hank told Ila he felt something like a politician stumping for missions, a sweet, slick-talker reaching toward pockets with his left hand while shaking hands with his right, interrupting the long established patterns of late fall living like some irritating disturbance in the weekly flow of things—television shows, high school games, December work schedules.

"You expect to play to packed houses every night?" Ila asked.

"It's having to do it. You have to do it. It's expected of you," he said. "That's what wears me out."

Thursday evening—a meeting with a youth group at a church in rural Minnesota, a town named Ashland. They were still an hour's worth of flat, pin-stripe country roads away.

"And all of this comes as a surprise?" Ila dropped the magazine she was paging through. "You mean to tell me you didn't expect that this job would be tedious?"

"What would you say if I'd tell the agency I'm not going back to the field?" he said, staring out ahead.

She let his question float by itself, as if it weren't really meant to be answered anyway.

He looked at her. "Well?"

"What would you think if I'd say I wasn't surprised?" She looked back at the magazine, licked her thumb, and continued paging.

"We'll take one of these vacant country churches out here. Great place to bring up kids, don't you think? You'd love it out here—" When he knew what Ila was thinking, those well-planted gaps in her conversation turned silly. He tried to anticipate what words she'd use to spit her sarcasm back at him.

"Drop me off in Chicago when you move," she said.

"Come on, honey. You couldn't live out here with me?"

As if offended, she slapped the magazine lightly on her knee. "Who do you want to answer that—your wife or me?"

"Remember when Dad called you a 'woman of to-day'? Remember that?"

"Your father would be happier if his blessed son married a girl just like dear old dad's." She rolled the magazine in her hands. "Maybe that's it, Hank. He treats you the way he does because of me. It's his way of trying to shoo-off his hated daughter-in-law."

Hank said he was sure that was the reason.

Ashland looked like any of a dozen prairie towns they had driven through all afternoon: false front businesses in square, inconsequential buildings up and down both sides of a two-block Main Street—a chain hardware store with tulip posters in the window, a grocery store, an insurance office, a bank, and a post office with a wall full of numbered boxes behind its broad front window. Several of the old-fashioned fronts were redone with modern looking elevations in an attempt to make the places look up-to-date—in the same way indoor panel-ling covers old wainscoting and turns a perfectly good room into something out of the 50's, Hank said. Maybe it was a little better kept, he told her, a shade more respectable looking than the other burgs down the high-way.

It was the supper hour in Ashland, and over half the diagonal parking spaces were lined with farm pick-ups, their back bumpers slapped with colorful stickers adver-tising seed corn, or singing the praises of farming, or hinting what incredible pleasures were the lot of women married to milkers. The cafe was named "Don's," and in the front window, just above the half-curtain which covered all but the balding heads of a few patrons inside, an old red neon light, with darkened spaces between the letters, flashed "HOME COOKING," as it probably did since the Great Depression.

"Nothing ever changes here," Hank said. "Not in a place like this."

Ila turned down the window a few inches as if to get a better look. "I knew a girl in college from Ashland. You remember her, Hank? Big, blonde. Gloria something— She was wild. Remember her? Ended up getting pregnant—"

"You grow up in a place like this and you just can't help busting loose sometime," Hank said.

"This is the kind of town where you want Tony to grow up?" she asked.

"So maybe there is no heaven down here below." He turned right slowly when he saw the denomination's triangular logo hung on a street pole.

"Little place like this worships their preachers," Hank said. "Whole town's history is written in chapters based on who was in the pulpit when. 'Started our annual Sunday School picnic when Rev. Vander Vander was here—' That's the way people talk."

"Maybe that's what you want out of life," Ila said.

"Man's got to get it somehow," he told her.

She crossed her legs and pulled her skirt tight over her knees. "There isn't a woman in the world that doesn't know what a man's got to have," she said.

Behind Main, the inside streets were all laid with well-kept curbs and gutters, and sidewalks. Even though it was December, the lawns still held enough color to make them attractive in the sun of late afternoon. Folks kept up their places well, two-story, red brick dwellings or old frame homes with spacious porches across the front, some with pillars, most of them painted in white or off-whites and trimmed in red or green or gray.

"You can tell there's Dutch folks in this place," Hank said. "Look at that."

He pointed at a more recently built home with stripes of marigolds up either side of the lot line, a circular display of impatience around the elm in the middle of the front yard, and window boxes overflowing with color hung from each front window.

"Don't be chauvinistic," Ila said.

"For pity's sake, Ila," Hank said. "Look for yourself. What other town have we been through today like this? There isn't a junked car in sight. No motorcycles parked on front lawns, no broken windows—"

"You miss that, don't you?" she said.

"The church must be down here somewhere—three blocks, the sign said."

"Hank, you miss that—that just-been-scrubbed Dutchness. I mean in the people in our church. You miss that down there—"

Beneath the trees along the road he could see what appeared to be an empty block up ahead. "This must be it," he told her.

"Answer me—" she told him.

He slowed almost to a crawl to pass the church. "Don't you? I mean, there are some times when I think a little bit of Dutch cleanliness would do our people a world of good. Don't lie, Ila—"

She sat there across from him with her hands crossed over her lap.

Ashland's Rev. Hutt combed his thick crop of gray hair just slightly over his ears. His wife, small and stylish in a red dress and white sweater tied over her shoulders, had perfect manners—"Let me take your coat, Mrs. Pietenpol . . . And this is the room where you can freshen up if you'd like . . . Maybe you'd like a sandwich and some tea now? . . . So, was it a nice trip?" In a

minute she had established herself as the kind of obse-
quious housewife who never stops telling you how much
she wants you to feel at home. She was the kind of
woman who intimidated Ila in a way that Ila especially
hated to be intimidated.

The preacher and his wife guided them very graciously
as they carted their suitcases through the museum of
knick-knacks in every corner of the house—coffee
spoons from a hundred tourist stops, arranged perfectly,
Hank guessed, as icons of the Hutt's self-image, the
trappings of folks who wished to display the fact that
they had travelled far and wide, beyond the limits of the
county lines.

"Let me help you with that, Ila—oh, what a pretty
name—Ila—oh, that's nice . . ."

It took ten minutes, no more, for them to settle in.
Hutt ushered him into the front room; the women
talked in the kitchen.

"So how goes the work in El Salvador, Hank?" Hutt
said. He was shy of fifty maybe, short and squat, the
kind of man who had, in all likelihood, stopped milking
cows when he was twenty-eight or so, when he very
likely mistook inveterate boredom for a call to the ministry. He sat, cross-legged, on the organ bench in the
living room, a bundle of thick thighs and calves.

It was almost the kind of question a Communist
would ask of a comrade, without the theology. "Good,"
he said. "Very good." There was really no other possible
answer. He could have tallied some figures—fifteen
adult baptisms, twenty-five presently attending pre-con-
fession classes—but Hutt was of the old school, just like
his father. Hank could see it in the way the man sat on
the bench instead of taking his own easy chair. Hutt
would think a factual recital too objective an evaluation
of the spiritual mission to Central America. His question
demanded a subjective answer—something like "fine
spiritual health." Hutt probably never heard of church
growth seminars, never thought of specific goals and

objectives as a management tool within the bride of Christ.

"I imagine it's a tough area to work," he said.

The whole living room was furnished with a kind of tidy sturdiness—nothing fancy, but nothing cheap: a long, nicely upholstered couch that looked heavy enough to hold a pull-out bed, a clean fireplace behind spotless glass, three thick easy chairs and a padded oak rocker beneath a pole lamp in the corner near a grandfather clock.

"It's not as bad as you might think. You read the headlines in the States, but the day-to-day life of most people in the city isn't affected all that much by the problems—by the fighting—"

"You know, when I came out of seminary I thought about missions a great deal, but our kids were at a bad age. I wanted them to grow up here." He stretched out his arms to each end of the bench. "Maybe that was selfish of me—" He nodded up at the family portrait on the piano. "There they are now—the youngest is still in college."

"We have a son—he's at his grandparents. But I know what you mean. The same thought's crossed my mind occasionally in the last year or so."

"It's not that there's no problems in a church like this. We got our share of sin too." Hutt cocked his head and winced, as if he'd borne more than his load of problems. "But I think you'll find our kids to be respectful. At least if they aren't, I'd be surprised."

"Kids will be kids anyway, I guess." He was happy Ila was being entertained in some other corner of the house. She would have shown him her teeth for such an empty response.

Mrs. Hutt leaned around the corner, making every imaginable effort not to be obtrusive. "Maybe, Rev. Pietenpol—may I call you Hank?—"

"Surely—"

"Maybe you would like to freshen up yourself a bit before seven?" Her face danced with smiles.

"Say, Hank, Anton Lubbers is coming over in an hour or so. You remember him, don't you?"

"I should, I suppose?—"

"He was born in Easton, and he knows your father, he says. Wanted to see you, so the wife asked him over later. Real nice people."

Hank didn't know any Anton Lubbers.

Just before seven he walked across the block to the church, a white frame thing, probably a century old, with a lit marquee out front facing the street. "First Covenant Church," it said. "Rev. S. Hutt, Pastor." *Pastor* was the word they used since *preacher* withered out of style. Seven years ago they were all *preachers,* Hank thought. Now they were all *pastors.* He had heard his father complain about the change.

"Sunday, December 9: 'Is There A Judgment?' " it said in bold, upper case letters.

Winter was coming on now. It seemed to have waited until Thanksgiving turkey turned into cold sandwiches. In four days of driving west the sky had slowly thickened into a cloudy blot that capped the bare prairie, and the constant rush of northwest wind bore through the gap between clouds and earth in great gusts. All day they had driven without sun, the rough-house winds pestering their little car, making him keep both hands on the wheel to keep it straight down the road.

He pulled the collar of his coat up around his neck and looked back at the church sign, thinking there was something sophomoric about sermons titled in rhetorical questions. When he looked around at the curtained windows adjacent to the church grounds, he guessed there was no one in a town like Ashland, Minnesota, who didn't already know the answer to the question posed by the sign. It just lacked the kind of zing to pull people in off the street. Of course, it was quite likely that Ashland had few people on the street anyway. So why would they advertise Sunday's sermon? For the benefit of the congregation? What did it matter what Hutt would hold forth on—they'd all be there. That's the kind of place Ashland was. Having been in town only a few hours, he knew it was no different from Easton.

A boy, maybe fifteen years old, met him just inside the door, the serious type. He recognized it immediately by the way his hair was locked down in a sweep over his forehead and in a straight shingle over his ears, held there for the evening by some greaseless hair tonic. He had the preacher's hair. Only one kind of kid would wear his hair in that kind of wave, cut and crimped like hay ready for the baler.

"You must be the missionary," he said, fingers stuck in his front pockets. The boy rolled on his feet, curling up from the soles of his feet to his toes—up and down, up and down—as if to get every inch out of his height.

"That's right," he said.

"It's a pleasure to meet you." And he recognized the boy, because in his hair, in his deliberate politeness, even in his excitement—this submissive courtesy he paid Hank—there was the image of his own youth, of himself, the president of the youth group in Easton, the boy the entire church quietly celebrated as heir to the highest communal blessings—no mere milker but some future kingdom worker, a *pastor.* Someday they'd call him a son of the church.

"The kids will be here in a while, I'm sure. It's a kind of thing they have—coming at the last minute like this. But they'll be here. We had an announcement at school to remind them." It was there in the way the boy looked at Hank, the unquestioning eyes, the unnecessary apology, the sense of purpose and calling that gave a fifteen-year-old the demeanor of a fifty-ish village mayor.

"Even if they don't come, you and I will have a good time talking," he said. "What did you have planned for me?"

The boy shrugged. "Nothing really. I mean, we just figured that you would have something to say."

Maturity—that's what the folks in church called the boy's great quality. That's what made him the boy most parents wanted their own kids to grow up into. "Be friends with so-and-so," they'd tell their own kids. "He's such a nice boy."

"That's a tall order," Hank told him. "Just talk about anything, eh?"

"I don't mean it that way, sir—not crazy like that. I didn't mean it—"

"I know," Hank said.

And the kids, they called his maturity something cute like "brown-nosing," or something worse, even more dirty. He was an adult in the clothing of an adolescent, an imposter, a kid robbed of a boyhood. The others likely saw him as a conscience. "He can handle himself so well," their parents would say, trying to prompt their own kids to pick up his attributes.

"Is there something maybe that you need?" he said.

"I didn't get your name—"

"Ah, I'm sorry. My name is Bruce Faber." His hand came out of his pocket on instinct, and he looked at it once, wondering whether it was awkward to shake hands this long after you met someone.

Hank squeezed it like his father would have. "Hank Pietenpol."

"I know you were born in Wisconsin," he said.

"You're right about that—"

"Dad said it."

Hank felt himself robed in the glories of the royal office of missionary. To the boy he was something of a celebrity. He could see it in the way the kid bowed and hear it in his slight stammer. "I suppose you're thinking of the ministry yourself someday, Bruce?" he said.

The kid laughed and looked away. "I don't know. I'm just a junior yet, and it seems like a long way ahead to have to make up your mind." Bruce pointed the way down the stairs at the back of the church. "Down here," he said, "this is where we meet." He snapped a light on around a dark corner. "Dad and Mom think it would be great, you know, but I don't know. I like farming a lot, but Dad says anybody can farm."

The old stairs shrieked as they walked down together. "Nobody's going to sneak out with these stairs," Hank said.

"We're getting a new church here, you know."

"No, I didn't—"

"I suppose not—I mean, down there in El Salvador you got more on your mind than to keep track of which church is building back home." He laughed at his own silliness.

The stairs wound around two corners and ended at the front of an assembly room that seemed specially designed for lectures. Maybe a dozen rows of wooden arm chairs, a dozen or so in each row, faced the front, where a heavily varnished table, maybe twelve feet long, ran parallel.

The boy pointed to the seats. "There's maybe a group of twenty or so that usually show up. Sometimes more. No ball games tonight, but we usually meet on Sunday night, so this is like an extra meeting."

"You have adult leaders?"

"They aren't coming." The boy tried to smile his way out of it. "You'll hear the kids when they show up— you'll hear them." The smile broke into a laugh, a you-and-I-smile-at-their-silliness laugh.

And that was another part of his character, that ready laugh, always jovial, as if one could be damned the moment his lips fell. In a boy like this one, a boy like Hank once was, a toothy smile documented one's righteousness.

"I was supposed to meet you at the door. They elected me President, so I get to meet the people who speak. You know—"

"Bruce," Hank said, "you remember when you decide what to do with your life, you remember that first of all comes the Lord. You be responsive to His call."

The boy nodded, and then looked away.

He wasn't telling the boy anything new, of course. It was just that he had to say those axiomatic things. They came to him in pulses, like meaningless lines of conversation—"the weather's been good."

"Mr. Pietenpol, what do you think?" He had the blue eyes, the sandy brown hair, but his features were fine, not so coarse, not so thick Dutch as Hank's had been when he was a boy. "I mean, you think I should be a preacher?"

He stood there like an empty glass waiting to be filled with communion wine.

"Why ask me?" Hank said.

"Well, you're a missionary, aren't you?"

"Sure I am." He felt speechless, even though his mouth was thick with stock answers. "Look, Bruce— that's something you and the Lord are going to have to decide. I can't really tell you much at all, except that the work is challenging, it's difficult, and it's full of big rewards. But the Lord's got to tell you if that's what He wants for you."

He knew it all sounded right, but he couldn't help thinking that an hour ago the boy wouldn't have known Hank Pietenpol from anybody else without overalls in Don's Cafe. And now the boy's eyes, blinking and unquestioning eyes, waited for some preposterous answer from a man he knew only as a missionary.

"You got to feel the call, Bruce," he said.

"I know that," he said, "but I can't guess what it's going to feel like when it comes." He looked down, almost embarrassed, as if this big decision threatened him like the black clumps of a storm hanging all afternoon on the horizon.

"Nobody hears it clearly, Bruce. Sometimes people just say things like 'hearing a call,' you know." He looked up over his shoulder for a second. "They make it sound as if it's all like Samuel—you know that story, don't you?"

The kid shook his head.

"It's not that way, usually." He leaned back against the table. "You got a long time, Bruce. Don't sweat about it yet. Live a little."

"It's just that next year I'll be a senior."

"You got a long time."

"Dad says I got to make up my mind before I go to college."

"I don't know—"

"He says it makes a big difference in courses and junk like that—"

"He's right, I guess."

"Well then, it's right in front of me—"

"You're too young to worry, Bruce. Believe me."

"But my father says—"

"There comes a time when you don't have to listen to your father." Hank ran it back through his head quickly. "I mean, you got to listen to yourself sometimes too. I think you'll know when the time comes. Don't let it bother you—"

"My parents want it bad, you know?"

"Sometimes you've got to understand parents, see? You've got to understand that mas and pas want things for their kids that they never had themselves."

A door opened upstairs and a babble of voices tumbled down the empty stairwell.

"They're here," he said.

They came in waves, four more after the first six, then two girls in fur-lined parkas, a couple of awkward boys leaning in towards each other as if they were afraid to be seen alone, and then a mixed group, more than a half dozen, the boys in open letter jackets, scarves hung around their necks, and the girls stalking the boys, chewing gum recklessly, the motion of their jaws the only outlet for all their energy.

"It looks like a good crowd," Bruce said.

"More than usual?" Hank unbuttoned his sport coat with his right hand.

"I never guessed this many, but a lot of them don't usually get out on Thursday night." He looked them over closely. "It'll be all right, though."

The first group settled in a row in the middle, and the rest filed in behind them, exchanging seats amid constant laughing, leap-frogging through the rows until it seemed each of them were satisfied. Three shy boys sat off on the left in the front row, and the sisters in matching coats slipped in to the right-hand side, somewhere near the middle.

"You want me to introduce you?" Bruce said.

None of them seemed too interested. They kept up their talking and giggling, craning their necks at each other down the row. "What do you think I should do?" Hank said. "I mean, should I just talk?"

Bruce seemed embarrassed by the missionary's hesitation. "Just do what all the missionaries do when they come here," he said.

"I do have some slides," Hank said.

Bruce said he didn't know if he could get a slide projector anymore. "If I'd have known—"

"That's all right. The slides aren't really for teenagers anyway."

Probably twenty feet separated him from the front line of kids, and between them lay a kind of buffer zone that seemed to bulge out like an over-filled milk carton. They were so far away.

More of them came in, indistinguishable teenagers in levis, sandy-haired, sometimes blond, unusually strong builds, thick shoulders and broad chests, clean faces, scrubbed cheeks, all neatly dressed, their hair shorter than kids wore it seven years ago. Hank guessed some were arm-wrestled into coming. "Go hear that missionary," their fathers had told them, kicking off their boots and hanging up their down vests in the back hall. "You planning on it, aren't you?" And it was, after all, a way out of the house. "Remember that blond?" Ila had said, "that wild one?" The girls were all pretty, fair-haired, fair-skinned, farm-healthy, popping up and down in their chairs.

"We even got some visitors from other churches," Bruce said. "That's something."

"And all of them just to hear about a missionary's story." Hank smiled when he said it, but the boy's Ashland eyes said that he wasn't, at fifteen, fully capable of irony.

Hank was afraid of them in a way—afraid of the impact of youthful force, of unrestrained energy, of youth that is America itself. Ganglike, they sat out there in the half-darkness, waiting for this man of the cloth to turn them all on. Yet, he knew they were betting against him. He wished he could talk to them in Spanish, because he was afraid of the language he hadn't used for seven years and the scrambled language of youth. Hector knew that language. Hank's first baseball coach—his mother said Hector had remarried now—that man could talk to kids in their language. A couple dirty words tossed in here and there. Hector knew how to talk.

One dream he used to have, in the old days in seminary, was when he worked with kids like these: the image of himself as a teacher standing up there in front of Babylon itself, trying to get the attention of a thousand kids but unable to do it, even with shouting or screaming above the level of their excitement. His angriest protests were wasted air, and his impotence scared the dickens out of him.

"I think maybe everybody is here now," Bruce said to the assembly. "Maybe we ought to get going."

They seemed not to mind the boy in the least, but it was nothing new. Hank had been through this business himself before, too many years ago, trying to settle the less mature.

"I said that maybe we ought to start now. It's already past seven." He barely raised his volume, and there was no appreciable effect.

"Hey!" It was one of the guys in a letter jacket who whistled and yelled. Then it was quiet. Like Hector would have done.

Bruce opened with prayer. He prayed well.

The church basement was lit by a half dozen ceiling lights, white globes, in two rows across the tiles, each of them circled with a dingy halo of dust at the bottom where no one, not even the tidiest Dutch janitor, ever cleaned. They had been hung there in another era, when electricity was an innovation, but today their glow was wholly inadequate, and the half-dark room too dungeon-like.

Bruce introduced him.

They quieted down, and it seemed odd. It surprised him. Occasionally he heard a word or a whisper or a muffled laugh, but from the minute he started talking he was surprised at the fact that he wasn't in a battle. It didn't appear they would bother him. The kid had told him that he thought it would be all right.

"How many of you have ever been out of this country?" he said.

No one raised a hand.

He told them how strange it was to live in a different culture, a place where everyday things you become used to at home—shopping, taking a shower, eating out— take on a completely different character. "Those things are like habits. A lot of our lives are habits. You don't even think about it, but a lot of our lives are habits. You don't even think about doing some things," he said, "because every day you do them, and you always have— you know, like eating Wheaties."

The polite girls in the front giggled. One of the boys looked down at his watch. Bruce sat alone but confident in the front, his arm stretched over the empty seat next to him, smiling as if behind him his own sweet children were sitting in rows.

Hank ranged back and forth, using his hands, remembering that variety and motion appealed to kids' attention. He described Salvadoran life—high schools, soccer games, things he guessed they might be interested in. He told them how popular music down there was pretty much a carbon copy of their own.

And their civility almost shocked him. Expecting a problem, he met only a curtain of quiet, hung, he guessed, from their respect. The way they tolerated him made him appreciate the purity and innocence of pastoral life in towns like Ashton. Ila should be here, he thought.

This was the way it was supposed to be, he'd tell her later—all attention and civility. They weren't any more than simple farm kids, but their sense of propriety was unexcelled. There didn't seem to be a rowdy soul in the room.

In the dim light he could barely see them clearly, but he knew they were listening, because it was quiet. He tried to explain where El Salvador was. No one appeared to know. The gap between them bothered him— four empty rows of chairs like a neutral zone.

"Most of the kids consider themselves Roman Catholic, but they know very little about faith. The church— some parts of it especially—seems very dead, little more than an institution, something ancient and huge that one is a part of simply because it's always been there." He knew it would be difficult to explain things clearly. "Maybe some of you have heard about a movement called 'liberation theology'?"

Bruce shrugged his shoulders apologetically, and Hank tried to spot some hands in the rows behind him.

He feared boring them. He could have launched into a full description of the way the church was renewing itself, but he knew it would be difficult to find a language to communicate theory in an exciting way. He glanced at his watch.

"The parts of the church that are alive are the people who try to make faith work in the lives of the people—" He couldn't do it without writing a lecture. "They try to make Christianity a force for change in the society." He felt as if he were speaking into a curtain. "They try to make faith relevant to the situations in which people are living—"

The sentences piled up at the edge of their silence.

"Maybe sometime you can ask your parents about 'liberation theology'—it's quite an issue with them."

He saw one kid poke the girl in front of him.

"I wish that all of you would consider missions someday," he told them. He tried to be sincere about it, even though it was something he was required to say on a furlough tour. "There is a real need for more workers, and the need keeps growing." He stood at the center, folded his arms over his chest. "Any of you thinking of going into missions?"

Two girls in the front looked at each other as if they weren't sure. The athletes' girlfriends giggled, their hands up in front of their faces. A kid in a university sweatshirt pointed at Bruce. "Maybe Faber," he said. "Ask him."

He didn't bother to check with Bruce. "None of you?" he said, looking for raised hands. Some shrugged their shoulders. One of the boys in a letter jacket yawned.

"Not one of you is interested in missions, and all of you have come to this church for your whole life—each of you?"

Someone cracked gum.

He hadn't sensed it before, because he had been thrilled by what he guessed was their respect, but it came to him slowly through their stony resolution. It was boredom written on their faces, traceable in their wandering eyes. They really weren't hearing the question, even though they appeared to be listening. Boredom was in their silence, in the deadness of a room where twenty minutes ago the volume of their energy had shaken the stairway walls; they were tolerating him. That's what it was. It was clear that they were giving him only their time.

Sixteen years of dead church practice had bullied them into sitting here and waiting for whatever patriarch had come in to finish a speech they had heard often enough before. "Do what they all do," Bruce had told him. Unwitting homage was knee-jerk with them, and it hardened them into four thick rows of cold cement. Dozens of circuit missionaries, dozens of Hank Pietenpols had hammered them with identical themes and the same lousy rhetorical questions—the challenge to serve—that had become, by this time, nothing but a cue that the speech was finally sneaking up on its long-awaited end. Their excitement, the energy of their emotions had, from the moment he started, simply found some place to rest for the space they allowed him, a half hour.

"I can't believe that none of you are considering mission work. Today it's a very broad field. I mean, not only ministers but doctors and nurses and construction workers, agriculturists too—anybody who can help struggling people live better lives—"

Bruce was smiling broadly.

"If none of you are interested in missions, then why are you here?" It seemed a logical question.

His question froze whatever restlessness had begun to show. Their attention drew a bead on him.

"Why on earth would you even come here tonight?"

They were too scared to respond now, he thought, but their silence urged him to keep on pushing.

"No one really wants to be here, do they?" He loved saying it. It almost made him laugh. "Nobody really wanted to come to hear me. Did anybody really want to come here tonight? Be honest!—" No response. He laughed outright. "If it would have been up to you, none of you would even be here, would you?"

He felt like a mountain in front of them. He felt huge.

"I got a real live captive audience here, don't I?" He put both hands up on his waist. "None of you really care."

He couldn't see Faber now, sitting directly to his right.

"Really—why are you here?" He tried to dull the edge of his own sarcasm, but to keep pushing them, far beyond the point where a hundred other missionaries had pushed them, beyond the comfortable words they had expected from him. "Why do you even bother to come?" he said.

The gap of empty rows stretched into flatland acres. He stepped between the chairs of the first row and looked at them, closer than he had before. "You—" He pointed at a girl flipping her hair out behind her jacket collar. "Why'd you come here?"

"I don't know," she said, glancing sideways at her friends. "You can get out of the house—" She tipped her head back and shook bangs out of her eyes, then looked at him and shrugged her shoulders.

"That's it for everyone here, I suppose, isn't it?" When he laid his fingers on the second row of chairs, he felt the scars carved into the wood. He looked down at the collected scribblings left from decades of guest missionaries, wondering what they had written in his half hour. Dark initials marred the writing surfaces; scraps of profanity stood out like billboard ads.

"What is this anyway? Maybe I should just go home. You don't really give a royal toot, do you?" It grew more and more silly, all of them sitting there, riveted to the old chairs, shook to the teeth with his charge.

"Why doesn't somebody say something? Talk back, for heaven's sake. Tell me you're alive anyway—" He stared at them. It was almost as if he wanted to fight them, to anger them enough to make them spit.

"I may as well talk to an empty room. Maybe these

chairs will talk back—" It was like a cave, he thought, just like a cave.

No one moved. No one had ever begged a fight with them before—not one of the circuit rider missionaries had ever squared off with them, challenged them the way he was doing. They were here to listen to him, the missionary. And everything he had said, everything he had guessed might communicate, was exactly the stuff everyone else—preachers from Bolivia, nurses from Taiwan, pilots from South American jungles—had told them before. He was "the missionary," and he had been giving them the perfect missionary line. Some official voice had been talking to them, not Hank Pietenpol.

"What are you anyway, some kind of play dolls for your folks or what?" He tried to make it a joke. "I mean, don't any of you know how you got in that front door—for Pete's sake? You just let yourselves get pushed around? Why are you here?"

"It ain't for this." The voice had come somewhere out of the back. Some of them dared to laugh. Their laughing made him smile, because the antagonism was so much better than silence.

"Who said that?" he said.

Give them the half hour they've allowed you, that's what the missionary would have done. Play the time clock for them. That's what they expected—even Bruce, sitting up in the first row somewhere by himself, wondering what on God's green earth was happening.

"Who said, 'Ain't for this?' Really, who said that?"

Their attention was fixed solidly; he could feel fear in their intense attention. Their faces appeared more clearly when he stood halfway back in the room, in the middle of the cloying smell of pretty perfumes and chewing gum.

"You know," he said, "in El Salvador there aren't many young people like you—not in my church. It takes guts to come to our church, guts of steel. Sometimes coming to our church breaks up families, see? Some parents will cut their kids right off if they show their faces in our church." He nodded at them, but they didn't understand. "They're different than you are. Down there, kids are different."

They were growing now. In his mind, they were getting bigger and bigger and bigger, so he tried to grab each of them, individually, with his eyes, while his mind scrambled for some truth, some moral to all of this, something his father would say to make this all into precept, because he knew that all of this tension had to lead them somewhere. There had to be meaning in it.

"Stand up on your own two feet, for pity's sake. Be strong."

Not much more than fear was registered in their faces.

He raised his hands. "I don't even know what to tell you. I haven't the slightest idea—"

"Maybe you ought to let us go home," one of them said, a boy in a letter jacket with a scarf hung around his neck.

"Not yet," he said. He could feel their attention clinging to him. *He* was speaking to them now, not the missionary; he had walked through the four empty rows to get there. "You know how hard it is for me to talk to you?" he said. "I'm not sure who is speaking. This isn't my speech, see? This isn't what I planned to say." Their expressions didn't change. "You don't understand me, do you?" He had to stop himself from yelling.

"You finished now, or what?" the boy said.

"No, I'm not done. You aren't getting away so easily tonight—just thirty minutes and you're free. No, sir. That's the way it's always been, hasn't it? That's the ball game. It's a regular pattern—you coming out here to church and listening to someone your parents line up for you. It's a ritual and a pattern and a habit." He walked up the row to the end of the aisle without facing them. "You kids are so young and it's a pattern already—"

"I don't get it," the kid said.

"You do too!—you're part of it already, even though you're just kids." He turned back to face them again. "You've already heard a dozen of us say the same things. It's nothing new. You're here because your parents say you have to be, so you give me your time. I'm the missionary after all—"

He looked down at his hands.

"What do you want from us anyway?" the boy said.

He knew that the truth was he hadn't a notion of where he was going with this. It wasn't one of his set speeches.

"You want us to sing now or something, or you want somebody to pray?"

Disgust came up in him like nausea. "I don't know— maybe it's just over—"

"Nobody here knows what you're talking about," the kid said.

"Don't you think I know that?" He knew he was too angry to carry this thing on. They were not capable of understanding what was going on, these kids. They wouldn't know for years yet. Some of them would never know. They'd live out all their years in perfect obedience. "I'm sorry. Really—maybe I should have just gone on with the mission thing—"

"You done now?" the boy said. "I mean, are you going to pray or something?"

"Just leave," he said. "I've been going on and on and you don't know what the heck I'm saying anyway. I don't know what got into me—"

The silence seemed mean.

"Don't you think you ought to pray?" Bruce said.

He put his foot up on an empty chair and pushed his fingers through his hair. "Go on—clear out. Maybe you'll remember me as the only missionary who didn't pray once he was finished with his ditty speech."

They seemed reluctant to leave at first, waiting for the boy who had dared to talk back.

"It's over," he said. "Go on. There's not a one of you anyway who gives two cents for any of this—"

The kid in the letter jacket rose and stepped out of the chair into the aisle. The rest followed, without even whispering. They walked by him carefully, as if he might suddenly take a swing.

Hank stood there facing the empty rows of chairs, as if some clear reason why he had said what he did would be carved into the desk top.

"You feeling all right?" Bruce said. "I can get you a glass of water or something—"

His hands were cold and sweaty. They felt dirty when he pulled on his coat.

Bruce said he'd stay behind and get the lights.

F I V E

Ten minutes of cold darkness outside cornered him with his own embarrassment. It wasn't that he thought he was wrong for standing up in front of them and holding forth the way he did. But outside the church, outside the crown of light at the front door, it seemed immodest, how he had acted. And he had no desire to see any of them again when he left the church, as if what had happened between them were a matter to be considered in hall-closet privacy, a quarter-hour slip, something to be regretted. Bruce Faber had left quickly.

And he couldn't judge whether he had won or lost because it was a different game he was in now. They hadn't really heard him, he knew that much. They would offer the next traveling mission show the same polite indifference they had showed him, all the while their young lives flowing like wet cement into a square section, pre-formed, like his own had.

The absence of speech had left him searching for an emerging voice. The baseball coach—Hector's odd snarl came back and the tangy twist of liquor in the air when they huddled around him before a game. He always sat on the bench and let the kids circle him. He told them about the other team as if there were some secret plan of attack—because he thought there was. You could see resolution in the way his arms flailed when he preached.

But somehow it was different with Hector's sermons. He spoke to them as individuals, as kids—and not just to their souls. They weren't children to Hector, not even ten-year-olds, and that's why his voice stayed with Hank. Straight talk from the man with empty beer cans rolling around on the floor of the back car seat. "This is what I am, you guys"—that's what his behavior and his language told them. "This is what I am—for better or for worse." No roles.

That was what he had tried to do, step out of his clothes and speak to them, and it had only made them uncomfortable.

It was cold now. In Easton, winter nights stayed warm from the heat of the big lake, a moonlit, speckled radiator, keeping the lakeshore marshland warmer than the inland woods and pastures. Five hundred miles west on the plains, the temperature dropped when the sun did, and the moment the western sky burned into red, cold air came over the prairie. The beginning of winter, December.

His breath came easier, smoother, in the cold over his face. He wanted to tell Ila, because he saw some things more clearly now. He had been forced into a character his father created—the missionary. It seemed as if all of it was to meet his father's ambitions and to avoid his displeasure—like Ashland kids, forced to come to church, the force already pushing so much into their lives they were blind to it. Those kids never even reached what the church called the age of discretion. Never.

At night nothing moved in Ashland. The sidewalk shone white in the dawning of the streetlights, but darkness covered the quiet streets, already at eight. At the preacher's the porchlight was on. They were waiting for him. Across the block he could see the house, a ranch style, newer than the church, probably built over the ruins of the old parsonage when some rich, retired farmer decided that his minister shouldn't be living in a house less dandy than the Lutheran's.

He worried about going to the Hutts' now, because he knew that for an hour, maybe two, he'd have to small talk, to pretend what happened at church was nothing more or less than what had gone on with every other circuited missionary in the century of history inlaid in the white frame church. He'd have to sit there and talk about El Salvador, maybe discuss theology or church politics, balancing some coffee on his knee, now and then eating a barful of calories. And always smiling, like a missionary, like blessed Mrs. Hutt.

He didn't want to go into the house. He wanted to tell Ila that the cold formality of the teenagers had been a mirror, that he saw himself scratching his own initials into the chair. So he stood there a half-block away, standing in the sugary frost on the church lawn, and he watched the house as if it might in a moment eclipse itself, the cold air waking him, settling him slowly. He stood in the middle of the grass until a car aimed down the street and turned through the parking lot, the long columns of headlights swinging over him standing alone like some odd fool.

An empty chair stood next to Ila, waiting for him, specially designated to have him whenever he returned, like the furniture of his past, already showing him what to do. Pastor Hutt sat on a padded folding chair, across the room. And Mrs. Hutt of the glowing face took his coat and hung it on the tree at the door. She could have been born in a town like Ashland, he thought. And there was the old man and his wife, both older than the preacher; the man was sitting on an easy chair, his knees clamped over each other, as if for half a century his legs had been folded in that position. He was bald, his face vaguely familiar. Hank couldn't recall the name, even though he remembered Hutt saying it earlier.

Ila slapped the back of his hand when he sat down. "Hank," she said, "this is Anton Lubbers. Do you remember him at all?" Her smile was bright and eager; she was oblivious to the church basement.

The old man held out his hand without rising from the chair, almost as if he meant it to be kissed. Hank walked over to shake it.

"I can't say that I remember you—"

"When you were born you was purple like anybody else's boy in Easton," the old man said. "No difference—even if today you are a missionary."

"He lived in Easton till what, Mr. Lubbers?—twenty-five years ago?—"

Hank went back to his chair.

"Twenty-five years," he said.

"—and he knows your parents very well. He told some stories already, Hank—" Ila rolled her eyes. "You wouldn't believe them. They're so funny. Things about your father."

"Hank Pietenpol, you grew up to be almost a man," Anton Lubbers said. "You're bigger than Wim and Corrie, but I remember Corrie's mother now—she was a moose. But not quite so big like you, though." He sat there in the chair like some aging monarch, moving only his forearms when he spoke. Maybe eighty years old, Hank thought, maybe even older.

The old man sat there appraising him. "So why did you leave Easton?" he said.

The man picked at his nose with his thumb and fore-

finger, then rubbed his hand beneath it from wrist to
fingertip. "This is an Easton boy, all right, Reverend," he
said to the preacher. "Most of them, they think that
when it is the end of time there won't be much change
down here below except some fancy angel coming by to
sweep the gutters every week. 'Why did you leave?'
Hank says. 'How can you leave?' they all said then,
twenty-five years ago. They don't know no better, Reverend. All them Easton people don't know no better."

Hank had to smile at the old man, because his playful
invective came from such a studious face, emotionless,
full of lines like an open box of pins.

"We moved because it was my wife what wanted to
come closer to her family," he said, without consulting
her. Hank realized he hadn't even seen a Mrs. Lubbers.
She sat there in the preacher's best rocker, both feet on
the floor, her toes aimed in slightly opposite directions,
rocking slowly, her fingers too busy with mending or
knitting. She seemed to be sworn to staying out of the
conversation, her mouth closed up tight beneath her
nose, as if she'd heard most everything the old man
would say time and again before, but she would, rather
painfully, tolerate hearing all the craziness again.

"Is that true, Mrs. Lubbers?" Ila said.

Her head tipped back a bit. "If Tone says it, then we
all know it's got to be gospel," she said. Talking didn't
stop the flurry of her fingers, but she did glance up
momentarily as if to underline the sarcasm.

Two minutes of conversation threatened to turn everything that had happened in the church basement into
a blurred memory, an odd, elusive dream left in the
darkness of the gravel lot across the road. He didn't
want to forget all of it so quickly; he wished he could
slip from the room and at least write it down somewhere, keep it fresh so it couldn't slip away in the rush
of humor from this old patriarch.

"What really happened was that we come in to the

folks' farm when they died, because Emma's sister's husband was too good-for-nothing to run it himself," Lubbers said.

"He's baker in town." Pastor Hutt aimed his remark at Hank, like a footnote in a continuing saga.

Even though he was born in an immigrant home, Hank recognized that brash matter-of-factness immediately. Non-immigrants frequently mistook it for callousness. Often, such brazenness was tactless, but it wasn't meant that way. It was simply—both in Lubbers and in his own father—a brutal commitment to nothing less than the truth, something immigrants often even expected in others.

By appearance, Anton Lubbers could well have been dead. His body remained motionless as he spoke, and his skin, from the draw in his neck up to his temples, hung in gray slats like pitched siding. Even when he wasn't talking his mouth fluttered, a nervous palpitation.

Hank could see that Ila loved every minute with the man; she sat in the corner of the couch, her legs sideways beneath her, and she watched him with an animated intensity. When she looked up at Hank, she flashed her eyes just slightly and shook her head, her way of saying that the old man was worth every minute of his time.

"So how did it go with the young people?" the preacher asked.

This was neither time or place for a full recitation of what had happened. He looked around quickly and smiled. "Good," he said. "They were very quiet. It went okay."

Hutt looked pleased and nodded at his wife.

"We have such fine kids in Ashland," she said. "Most people who come here are amazed at how well-behaved they are—" Hank thought the woman made a perfect preacher's wife.

"Years ago it was worse," Anton Lubbers said. "We were worse years ago. You can believe it."

Lubbers could make a statement stop conversation

like some catchy ad line. "Years ago it was worse," he had said, but the line stayed there like the bright first line of a great sermon, and the rest of them, speechless, waited for more.

"I remember," he said, "we had once this preacher named Menno Haan. That name means *rooster* in the Dutch. You know him maybe, Reverend Hutt? Or would he be before your time?"

Hutt shook his head, waving off the suggestion that he could be so old.

"That was the ugliest minister I ever saw."

Ila laughed. Hank could hear her breath hesitate.

"Jug handle ears, you know." Lubbers' hands framed the sides of his head. "And here, this big Adam's apple." He lifted his chin and poked his own around. "And in them days we always sat way in the back of the church, all the kids did. That was before your time in Easton, Hank. At night we was all of us back there in the rows, one beside the other. Sometimes the preacher stopped preaching because things got so rough with all of us back there. 'Now behave,' the Dominie would say. Your pa too, Hank, God bless him. He was no better himself them days. You get some of us old ones together and we can tell some stories."

"—You have to tell Hank about the dance," Ila said. "Maybe later. He's got to hear that one—"

Lubbers nodded at the interruption. "So it was one night when we were back there. That night we acted pretty decent in behavior. This Dominie Haan, he was not so blessed with a voice either, you know. Oh, he was so ugly, too, but he had this kind of scrawny voice—half crow and half rooster maybe. So it's finally to the end of the sermon and all we have to go anymore is the song. That's what makes us restless too, you know. We are getting out now once finally and into the buggies.

"So the Dominie stands up in front of all of us and we watch him because we're waiting for it to be over now— the worship. Yeah, I know that's not so nice either, but then you know how it is with kids. 'Now ve shall zing,' he says, cause he has that thick Dutch yet, 'Now ve shall zing auf nummer 122,' it was. So there he is, so ugly and he leans back like always, and we see that big jumpy ball of Adam's apple. And always he does this when he reads the words over, he leans back, you know, because he gets himself all struck with the rapture of it. 'Ve shall zing auf nummer 122—"Lord, Like a Pelican I stand!"' he says, just like that. He said *pelican* instead of *publican*."

Ila held her head in both hands, and Pastor Hutt leaned over on his elbows, laughing. His wife wiped a tear from her eye with the handkerchief she clutched in her fist.

The old man barely moved in his chair. "And there we were. Your father too, you know. I remember. And that bench just almost cracked in on us because we laughed so hard. 'Lord, Like a Pelican I Stand,' he said, you know—with his head way back as if all of the words were going straight up to heaven." Lubbers stopped to gaze up at the ceiling. "That man looked just like a pelican, see—that Menno Haan."

Hank couldn't help but laugh. The church basement and the kids and his own stumbling performance still churned through him, but the old man broke the edge of his anger—if that's what it was he was feeling. Maybe it was fear. Maybe it was embarrassment, seeing too much of himself in the timidity of the kids. He tried to bring it back.

Ila grabbed his wrist as if to balance herself.

"So maybe a dozen times before I heard him tell that one," Mrs. Lubbers said, reaching down and into her carpet bag. "And every time anyway I have to laugh." It rolled up from her stomach and shook through her shoulders, then came out quietly but audible, as if it were a massive bubble of air.

"You should have been here before," Ila said. "They're really something."

Tone Lubbers smiled—you could see it hint at the corners of his lips—and his jaw kept moving in a slight circular motion, as if he were rolling another story between his teeth.

"Pelican," Hutt said.

"Sure, *pelican,*" Lubbers said. " 'Lord, Like a *Pelican* I Stand.' Right out loud we laughed, back there in the last row of the church. Right out loud, and in the middle of the service, us younger ones. That don't happen no more, young people laughing in church like that."

"Thank goodness," Mrs. Hutt said. She tugged at the hem of her skirt, inching it over her knees.

"I could tell you worse things too," Lubbers said.

"No sense in remembering things that should better be forgotten." Mrs. Lubbers drew in a deep breath that sounded much like a warning.

"What you think about the Klaas Alderink story, Ma?" he asked.

She didn't really say yes or no. She sat there stiff, her fingers motionless, and looked at her husband as if he were the subject of an experiment.

"No, maybe not," he said. "It don't need to be brought up again."

The conversation gapped momentarily, but even the silences stretched tight as well-staged pauses under the old man's supervision. Even the silences belonged to him. Hank had nothing to say. He sat there like the others and waited, anticipating whatever narrative the old man would spin next.

"So now you are in El Salvador, Hank?" he said.

Hank tried to smooth the smile from his face.

"I see your picture sometimes around. I don't know— in church somewhere." He folded his hands in front of him, both elbows over the arms of the chair. "And always I say to Etta here, 'Etta,' I say, 'that boy I remember from the day he was a baby this big.' " He stretched his arms out as if he were telling a fish story.

She nodded.

"And your father. I know Wim too. Maybe he talks about me sometimes—but maybe not, too—"

Hank wondered if the man's jaw fluttered when he slept.

"So what is news in Easton?" Lubbers said.

Hank looked at Ila. "Don't know, really. We've been home for only three days."

"Not much of anything anyway, I suppose. Not much different here, either."

"Different than what?" Hank said.

"Just different. Pretty much the same all the time— that right, Reverend?" He held his hands up in front of his face, stringy fingers and big round knuckles. "It's not much different in Ashland. Pretty much always alike, things are. We could use sometimes a man like your father."

"Why do you say that?" Ila said.

"You know Wim Pietenpol, Reverend?" Lubbers said.

Pastor Hutt shook his head.

"In our church we have no saints, but if we were Roman, Wim would be the one—that I know." His mouth closed up tight for a moment. "But he is human too, your father. Maybe you never heard the story of the meeting in church, Hank. It was Depression then—the meeting when he told the story about the man on the cliff. That one you know, I'm sure, Hank—"

Ila pulled her legs tightly beneath her. "I didn't hear it," she said. "Tell it, please—"

Anton Lubbers tipped back his head and closed his eyes. His nostrils flared when he inhaled. "It's back in here someplace," he said. "But what it was anymore, I'm not so sure. I don't know again now why your father told that story—"

"No faith," Mrs. Lubbers said, toying with her needles. "It was for no faith. The church had no faith—"

"Ja, ja, that was it. Faith was the reason. Ja, Etta has it there. I remember. Some of them in Easton church says, 'No, we can't do it'—what it was I can't remember now.

Maybe it was church quota or budget. There was some who said, 'We have no money to pay the budget anymore. We can't pay.' I don't know now just what it was again, but it was a fight in the church, and some said, 'No, we can't,' and the others say, 'Yes, we must.' One of those kinds of fights—what it is you should do against what would be so easy and what you'd like." He stopped and nodded, as if he had finally pulled the memory from some dusty file.

"So what happened?" Ila said.

"There was a fight, you know, this kind of argument; 'yes, we must' against 'no, we can't.' This kind. So Wim he stands up, and he is a young man yet then in '35—maybe not even thirty years old. But he has this way with him—ha, you know that too. You should see this man once, Reverend. He has this way, you know. People just listen to him. Maybe it is in those shoulders. 'You know,' Wim says—and he stands up—such a young man to talk at the meeting of the congregation. 'This reminds me of a story,' he says."

Lubbers stopped and laughed. "Never will I forget this either. It was something. 'This is like a story,' Wim says. 'Once there was a man who got himself on a cliff and there he hung, from maybe a branch this big that he was holding onto with one hand.'" Lubbers drew a circle with his fingers, maybe six inches wide. "'And if he lets go he will die for sure, because he is hanging there and holding on with just one hand.'"

He pulled his fingers over his lips, trying to bring back the exact lines. "Well, you know the people are listening, because in a church meeting nobody ever tells stories. Usually, it's just a big fight. But I remember. I was nervous a bit, because there is this young man, Wim Pietenpol, telling a story in front of the whole church, and the people don't know quite how to take it yet. Maybe someone should tell him to just shut up—that's what we thought." Lubbers stopped for a second and let slip a laugh.

"But Wim tells his story: 'So the man yells, "Help, help, help—will someone up there help me?" ' Wim says. 'And the man hears from above this voice, maybe a low voice what says, "This is the Lord God Almighty up here on the edge." ' "

The old man stopped, and his eyes flashed like quarters.

Ila started laughing.

"And none of us know what is going on—we don't know yet what we have to think, because the way he says it sounds almost like he's making fun of the Lord— you know, the Lord speaking to this dying man like that. But sure it can't be a barn joke to tell in church, we think. So nobody knows how to take it yet.

"But your father goes on again: 'And the man says, "Lord, you must help me or I'm going to fall to my own death!" And the Lord tells him, "Just let go of that branch in your hand." That's what the Lord says. "Just let go of that branch—go on."

" 'So the man, he thinks to himself how if he lets go he will smash his body on the rocks way down in the valley. And the Lord says again, "You must let go once. Just trust me. Do you trust in the Lord? You just let go—trust me," the Lord says.' "

Tone Lubbers stopped to scratch his eye with his knuckle.

"It was something, Reverend. Wim stands up and all of us are watching him. 'So the man looks up above,' Wim says, 'and the man says, "Maybe there's somebody else up there to help me," he says, because he doesn't trust the Lord God Almighty.' "

Lubbers shook his head as if it were one of the great moments of his own life. "And then Wim pounds his fist down on the bench in front of him. 'Too often with us it is always the same—we don't have enough faith,' Wim says.

"And then he sits right down. He looks like maybe he

is angry or something. It was something you can't forget."

Hutt tried to muffle his laughter with his hands.

Ila seemed almost shocked, her hands up on her cheeks. "And the people laughed?" she said.

"Oh, no. No, no, no—because Wim looked so angry. No one dared to laugh. And it was the end of the whole fight, right there. Wim ended it, and he was just a young man yet. Usually the young men don't talk much in those days." Lubbers inhaled heavily through his nose. "Maybe that's why I remember that story. But no one laughed. You can't tell a joke in church back then."

Hank had never heard the story. It would have been unusual, out of character, for his father to have reminisced in that way. He wasn't the type to say how he had once stopped an argument with a good story.

But it bothered him to admit that he had never heard it before, because it was as if there were parts to his father's life that he didn't know, that he couldn't know. It seemed almost strange that Wim might have a life apart from his life as Hank's own father. He felt jealous at not hearing the story before.

"But you, Hank," Lubbers said, "I remember you looked just like the rest when you were a baby—that purple face. No one could ever guess you would end up called to be a missionary. I remember how you looked as a baby. You remember, Etta?"

All of them watched her, waiting for her to nod her head. Mrs. Lubbers said she remembered.

"Tell us some more, Mr. Lubbers," Ila said. "What else do you remember about Hank's father?"

The man's jaw stopped fluttering when he looked up, his eyes sweeping back and forth across the seam of wall and ceiling across the room above the couch. It was impossible to think this man could have been a boyhood friend of his father, or that his father had ever had a boyhood. Anton Lubbers. Anton Lubbers must have been thin as a boy, with bushy hair and black shrub eyebrows. His thin lips curved slightly down, an ironic deadpan twist.

"I remember," he said, "I remember this, too. I remember how happy he was—and Corrie too—when finally they learned that she was *in verwachting*—you know, when she was going to have you. They weren't younger people anymore either. But this you know already, I'm sure."

Pastor Hutt asked how old they were.

"In the forties. In those days it was more common, but they still were not young anymore—"

"You're an only child?" Hutt said.

Hank nodded. He didn't like that grin across the preacher's face or that omniscient nodding, because he'd seen it so often before, as if the tag served to answer a volley of questions about him.

"What I remember is how the whole church was happy. And your mother, she hid it in the old-fashioned way when it started to show, but she didn't want to hide it, not really. You could see it, how happy she was. You know how they say that about mothers in the family way—how they glow. That was like Corrie. It was in her eyes that she didn't want to wear those coats to cover her, because she was so happy, even though there was others her age who were already grandmothers." Lubbers raised his hand in the air as if he were gesturing for peace. "I think maybe we could have thanked the Lord in church when you came into the world, Hank. The dominie could have said it in his prayer, but in them days we didn't do those things. But everybody in that Easton church was happy for Wim and Corrie. You remember that, Etta?"

She remembered.

He felt trapped. For a moment he wished his own pulpit were out in front of him so he could control things. It was an odd feeling, as if there in front of all of them were an open scrapbook of childhood photos, himself lying naked on an infant's blanket. It was his own life being examined through old stories tumbling out carelessly, just so many cute little anecdotes. They sat around him thumbing through his life, picking his father off a counter and turning him upside down in their fingers.

"It was such a surprise?" Ila said.

"They were old already. They had never had any children—"

Hank remembered how his mother used to say it was like Abraham and Sarah. She would say it with a smile on her face, because it wasn't necessarily proper to be cute with God's Word.

"No one worried about their age?" Ila said.

"It was different then. Women had babies until they stopped. That's the way it went." Mrs. Lubbers twirled the needles. "No one worried for them because they had such faith, both of them—Wim and Corrie. It was as if this boy was a miracle, so no one worried about them."

Hank felt as if he were a child with a rattle in his fingers, sitting right here in the middle of the rug. He had no entrance to the conversation. Unwillingly, he watched them.

"But you know already the rest of the story, Hank," Lubbers said. "That other part. You see that shows it too—why you were such a blessing. But you know that part already, I am sure—"

"What do you mean?" he said.

"I mean what it was that happened early in life for Wim and Corrie. You already know about that—"

The urge to know what this old man knew numbed the stinging embarrassment of his own ignorance.

"What are you talking about?" Ila turned towards Hank. "What on earth is he talking about, Hank?"

"I mean, you know what it was that happened with your folks. Some time they must have told you that.

What happened when they were younger and when maybe they were foolish—"

"What?" Ila said. "I don't know. What happened?"

Lubbers checked with the preacher, as if he needed the man's permission to go on. He seemed unaccustomed to his own uneasiness. "Maybe I shouldn't say this. I don't know. I thought for sure you knew already. That you heard by this time. I thought sure Wim told you." He glanced at his wife, as if some sign would appear.

She seemed set to work in her fingers. Sternly, she cleared her throat.

Lubbers knew he had gone too far. There was no going back anymore. "I thought you knew, of course," he said. He looked around again, and when he spoke his tone had changed, lowered in pitch. "You had once a sister. She would have been much older, maybe twenty years. I'd have to count. But she died in childbirth. She was born too soon." He stopped, his fingers pressed together in front of him. "I'm telling you this now for the first time, you say?"

"I didn't know," Hank said.

"What happened?" Ila said.

Lubbers looked up slowly. "She died in the hospital just after she was born. It was maybe a fever or the flu. Babies died then, more often. And this one—she would have been your sister—she was just born too early. Not strong enough to live. And your mother too, you know. Your mother was never a healthy woman either."

"You never knew that before, honey?" Ila said.

Hank disliked Ila's questioning, her prying.

"Why didn't they tell you?" she said. "You would think they would tell you something like that. My goodness, it must have torn Mom apart. Why keep it from you?"

There were no answers anywhere and that's why he disliked her. She knew more about him now than even he knew. He didn't have enough time to think it through, what it meant—this business about a sister. He felt controlled, in Ila's hands.

"I can't imagine why they wouldn't have told you that," she said. "Was there something odd about it? You know, Mr. Lubbers?"

Silence did not fit Anton Lubbers well. He sat straight in the chair, one knee hung over the other, and twitched his shoulders as if he were irritated by something at the small of his back, his lower jaw always fluttering.

An emotion Hank didn't recognize welled up in the back of his throat, then reached up gently and pulled at his eyes from behind. He wanted to cry—for his father he wanted to cry. To them, Wim Pietenpol was already dead, unable to be here and explain it all—why they had never told him about this baby.

"Some things maybe we ought not to remember at all," Lubbers said. He closed his mouth.

Ila put her hand over Hank's wrist. Hank sat as if in stone.

"You got to say it, Mr. Lubbers," Ila said. "We want to know. Both of us want to know."

"You too, Hank? Is it something you want to know?" Lubbers waited.

"Of course he does," Ila said.

In quick passes Lubbers' eyes shifted over them. "It isn't so good, me telling you this maybe, but the girl was born too early and conceived out of wedlock. Wim and Corrie had to stand up and confess in the old way, you know—in front of the whole church."

"You remember that too?" Ila said.

Lubbers coughed into his hand. "Some things there are that you shouldn't remember, but—it's always that way—it's those things you don't forget so easy."

Hank didn't want to see Lubbers anymore, because the whole thing had become dirty now. Wim and Corrie took it all, undeserving, both of them sitting home now with their grandson. Here in some Minnesota prairie town, these people split them open.

"It must have been sad," Ila said. Hank refused to look at her, even though he could feel her eyes on him. "What they used to do in church was so cruel—"

"Your mother showed it in the face that she was *in verwachting*. Like with you it was. And I remember my mother crying there on that day, because it was not common, both of them up there together, you know— both of them so strong, and just married so short a time. But it was something, all right. Maybe that is why that picture sits up here yet in my head. The church—together— we forgave them their sin. That's what I remember too, even in the way we sang just afterwards."

"I just can't stand the thought of it," Ila said.

"No, it was forgiveness, what we felt for them—for Wim and Corrie. It was forgiveness. I remember my own mother crying in the buggy after church. Crying. But it was more too. Forgiveness. They were so strong when they stood up there, Wim and Corrie. It was like sin—it was like sin was there and then in comes forgiveness, like a wave into the church. All of it was so strong that it was like a testimony. That whole Easton church too was strong. The whole church. Forgiveness comes, you know, like a big wave in there." Lubbers' smile spread across his closed lips.

"You never knew any of it, honey?" Ila said.

He felt cheated. Of course he didn't know. "No," he said. "I didn't know anything." It would have made a difference. Right away he was sure that knowing would have made a difference.

"I can't imagine why they wouldn't tell you," she said.

"Maybe there was no need, Ila," he said, "there was no need to say anything, to uncover all of that." He stared at her. "What good would it have done me to know? I don't know one good reason. How would it have changed my life?" He sat back and pushed his fingers through his hair. "Would it have saved my soul?" He tried to swallow his anger. He looked at her, at the side of her head. "My word, Ila, you think you know absolutely everything there is to know about your parents? You think there aren't some secrets you don't know?" Wim shouted in his mind, pointing his finger. "We've all got secrets, Ila." He looked down at his hands. He could feel the pulse bounding through his wrists.

"Wim and Corrie Pietenpol," Mrs. Lubbers said. She kept knitting, always looking down. "Wim and Corrie Pietenpol. When my husband gets talking serious, always he talks of Wim and Corrie Pietenpol, Hank. When the preacher asks us to come over tonight, Tone, he says it is Wim and Corrie's boy." She dropped the needles. "I could tell you once, Hank—when we had five children and the oldest one just nine. I can tell you how your mother gives me in church one Sunday twenty-five dollars stuck in a birthday card. 'For you,' she says. 'Wim says you should buy yourself something nice, maybe a new coat—just for yourself.' And not even my birthday." She pointed at him. "I could tell you more, but me, I don't talk so much like Tone."

"If Etta talked so much as me," Lubbers said, "for us, years ago it would have been over."

Together, they sat around what seemed to Hank the edge of some long, unfinished highway, pushing right out the front door.

He remembered a time when they had come out of an unpicked cornfield without seeing a pheasant. Hank pumped one shell out of the magazine, and the shotgun went off, the barrel pointed down and away from him. The shot pattern scraped up roadside gravel less than a foot from his father's toes. Wim Pietenpol swore at him. He rarely swore. "You could have shot me." Hank was maybe thirteen years old. And the mess of gravel there, shame and guilt commingled, a sense of letting his father down, along with the fear of almost having hurt him.

"You can't be so reckless with guns," his father had said.

But he couldn't look into his father's face. "You hear

me, boy?" Wim yelled. "You understand?" He shook
Hank at the shoulders until Hank raised his head and
showed his father the tears.

"You got to be careful," Wim said, backing away, his
hands up like a fighter in front of his face. It had been
quiet that day in the car all the way home.

And the woods came back to him now, his terror at
the idea of Wim Pietenpol lying there bleeding in a cold
bed of snow. And the image of both of them, younger
than he had ever known them, standing up in front of
the old church, their faces down—then up, forgiven.

Hank had never sat with them in their kitchen and
drank coffee, because they didn't admit him to that
world. But he didn't want it, either. Maybe he didn't
really know them, he thought. Maybe one never really
knows his own parents, not as human beings anyway, as
anything less—or more—than father and mother.

"So tell us once about how it is in El Salvador," Lubbers said.

S I X

I t was just after one when the call came; he read the
time on the digital clock on the dresser, its bony
computer numbers blinking down over the bed.
Light in bedrooms bothered him more than Ila for some
reason. For an hour he was tempted to pull the plug on
the glare of the clock's cold light. But when Ila fell asleep
quickly and he was left to himself, the stick-like numer-
als' shifting seemed rhythmic.

From the church basement, he had come into the cold night hating his father. Then, in the span of a short conversation, he had felt pity for them, for a time that he could barely imagine. Something inside him wanted to argue with Lubbers, tell the old man that the whole pregnancy was a mistake, that it really hadn't happened.

His own mind stretched tight, trying to get the whole image of his father clearly in his mind. Never before, not in all those years so many miles away, had he tried so hard to determine what the old man had done for him, where he had pushed and pulled and what his own reaction had been.

He had told Ila outright just a few seconds after they were in bed, "Maybe I've had it with El Salvador." It was the one idea that seemed somehow right in his mind.

But she was in no mood to be serious, still brimming with Lubbers' finest lines, so she barely responded. "No kidding," she said. Laughter and surprise, something close to shock, still cracked through her voice. The mattress on Hutt's guest bed leaned them toward the middle; they lay on their backs, wedged together. "Anyway," she said, "you've said it before, so it doesn't shock me. Nothing shocks me, for that matter—not after the story about your folks. Can you imagine them making love somewhere in a buggy? I wonder where it happened."

Motionless, he remained deliberately silent for what he regarded as her childish thoughts. Dredging up some half-century old desecration seemed the worst kind of clothesline gossip.

"That Lubbers guy—" Occasionally she giggled through an echo of the old man's voice, but it was half past twelve when she finally turned away from him, and he heard her sleep, the soft clicks in her throat when her breath shifted between her nose and mouth.

Not to return to El Salvador was a fundamental decision. It seemed just and right. Going back again, remaining a missionary would be living off the accrued benefits of a role—even a confession—long ago determined for him. Simply rolling along with things now would be like admitting publicly that he had never realized that being a missionary was not his own decision. It seemed right to divest, if for no other reason than to document his own liberation. He wasn't the same person anymore, because finally he felt cut loose from a mold it had taken him thirty years to grow up out of.

The square-cut digits flicked through the minutes, the circular 3s right-angled into piggy-back boxes, and the diagonal arm of the 4 spread back to a parallel, vertical line.

Alone in the dark, quitting the mission seemed right to him. He had to quit because he had never really exercised any option in the first place. Not like Bruce Faber. Not even like that boy. He could have spent some classic lines on Bruce Faber: "Wait for God's call" or "Know the Lord's will"—some glory like that. But he himself had never fought with the boy's questions, because what he would do and what he would be had been laid out broadly before him, like a swath of prairie flatland without end. Once, years ago in seminary, there had been some question about whether or not it would be missions, but nothing soul-rending, nothing agonizing. Decisions, real decisions, he had never made. Thirty years of his father's admonitions had bullied him down familiar paths, shaped him, his vision of himself and his world, as effortlessly as lake swells smooth straight-cut lumber into driftwood tresses.

He was always the best of the young people. He never carved one cuss word. Hank Pietenpol had never made fun of kids like himself. He had never referred to his father as his "old man." He had never really stood apart from his father's exacting designs for him, never really measured himself by any standard other than the one mirrored in a lifetime's scrapbook of occasional homilies.

At one o'clock the phone rang in the kitchen. Mrs.

Hutt's muffled voice stumbled through an indistinguishable phone conversation. He heard the phone being set down on the table, house-slippered steps down the hallway.

"Hank," she said, knocking, whispering, as if somewhere in the house there were children who shouldn't be awakened. "Hank, it's your father. You had better speak to him."

It was four minutes after one on the digital.

"Hank," Wim said, "your mother is dead."

"Mom—"

"She died already three hours ago maybe. She just plain died. Just like that—bang—she was dead. She put Tony to bed tonight, and she comes down and sits here in her chair, and just like that her head goes down to her shoulder and she was gone. So fast."

"Did she—"

"So the ambulance comes too, but I know she was gone right away. The doctor says, 'Massive,' he says. 'It was a massive heart attack.'"

During the silence, Hank felt a struggle for confidence in his father's uneven breathing. "We'll come home tonight yet, Dad," Hank said.

"No hurry. Tony is asleep, you know. He slept right through all of it, the whole works. He doesn't know any different yet. I thought maybe to bring him to Edna Huitsing, across the alley in the back, but maybe now I need him in this house—"

"Dad, Ila and I will—"

"You listen. You start in the morning, Hank. Let Ila sleep. Now?—it would be silly. To start now would be foolish."

The Hutts had mounted a foot-square bulletin board next to the phone. A yellow note, stuck there by a thumb tack, said, "Lettuce and mayonnaise."

Wim inhaled audibly, deeply. "Without her it won't be so good for me, Hank. Nearly fifty years for us—already it was nearly fifty years, you know."

"I'm glad Ila and I are here now, Dad—I mean, I'm glad we're here on furlough."

Wim's silence assented.

"Well, maybe already we talked too long like this, long distance. And tomorrow you will be home too." The pause stretched uncomfortably.

"Dad, I'm sorry," Hank said. Ila was there now; he felt her hand on his arm. "We'll be home quick tomorrow."

"You make sure now that you tell all those churches that are expecting you to come yet. Maybe when you get home we can do that, sit and call—"

"Don't worry, Dad. I can take care of that."

He heard his father's laugh brush the mouthpiece. "She's gone now, Corrie is. I got to do this all myself now. And you too—you got to do things different now, Hank." It was as if he could trace the leaps his father's mind was making through the silences. "And tomorrow I have to make breakfast for me and Tony—"

"Dad, we'll leave yet tonight. Ila's awake now—"

"You tell Ila. It's her mother too that's gone."

"Sure, Dad. Of course."

"Maybe already we talked long enough," Wim said.

Hank nodded as if his father was standing there at the sink. He wound the cord through his fingers.

"I have to tell you yet too now how good it was for Tony to be here with her. Like Eli and the baby Jesus in the temple it was with her. Five days with her own grandson—and I'm not making light of the Word of God either. She was ready to die, Hank. Your mother was ready to go. Sometime I think if I had faith—of what she did—even half, I would be as strong."

"Sure, Dad, we can talk tomorrow. You try to get some sleep."

Wim's shock was pressed into the gaps in their conversation. His fear fluttered through the unusual quiet like some night bird flying back and forth through the crown of light beneath a street lamp.

"And it's too bad, you know, that you have to cancel

all of that. Those churches out there, they look forward to you coming, I'm sure—"

"It's nothing, Dad. Really, it isn't. Don't be so crazy about it."

"What do you mean, 'crazy?' You know, you have an obligation to those people, and now you have to break it. Everyday they don't hear missionaries in some of those churches."

Hank let it pass. Ila already knew somehow; she stood there quietly beside him in the silence. "You just get some sleep now, Dad," he said. "Just get back in bed and try to sleep—"

"But you stay there—you hear me? You stay there in Minnesota and you can start out in the morning. That's smart."

Hank said he would.

"So what is an extra few hours now? I know how that goes. Some time in the morning, then the eyes get so heavy you can't work anymore to keep them open."

Ila held his arm. She knew.

"Too long already I've talked. You know—the bill—" Wim drew another breath slowly.

"Get some sleep yourself now, Dad," Hank said. "You hear? Maybe a glass of wine or something."

"Sure," Wim said. "I can sleep now. Corrie is dead, and there was no suffering at all, nothing."

"Tomorrow we'll be there—"

"Ja, and you be sure to drive slow now. No reason to hurry, because there is no one who is going to go somewhere now. Just drive safe, Hank."

"Sure, Dad." He waited through the gaps in the conversation, listening for the phone to click.

"There was no suffering. She walked right out of her chair here and she walked right into the bosom of her Lord. But I will tell you tomorrow about that—"

Hank waited.

"You drive careful, Hank," Wim said.

"Sure."

"And you tell Ila—"

"Ila knows. She's right here. Maybe if I called the preacher over there—"

"Already he was here and gone. I know already everything he tells me anyway. But maybe it is a good experience for him. Maybe two or three funerals he's had in his whole pastorate, you know? But he did it good, Van Gaalen did. He did all right—"

"Get some sleep now, Dad."

"Ja, sleep will be good. And tomorrow I have to get breakfast myself, you know." Wim sniffed twice. "Tomorrow already you will be here too. That's something. So far away and tomorrow you will be here already. Maybe ten hours it will take, Van Gaalen says."

"Ten hours."

"Good-bye, Hank." The click of the receiver bit the line.

Ila pressed herself into his side, pulled him into her. There was only one light on, a recessed bulb hidden behind a woodwork facing over the kitchen sink.

Through the early morning darkness they almost owned the interstate through southern Minnesota. Here and there some hustling livestock hauler passed them doing seventy at least, sweeping the very light snow from the left lane into white froth in the middle of the highway, but otherwise it was quiet until dawn made the clouds glow in the east.

"Maybe we ought to stop for something," Hank told her.

"I don't know if I could sit in a restaurant right now," Ila said. "Seems like we ought to be back there for him."

"Maybe we can find some kind of drive-thru. Pick up some donuts or something."

Twenty miles from the border, they drove down off

the prairie flatland and followed the hills along the wide spread of the Mississippi, the jutting bluffs standing up above the river like balding scalps clearly visible beneath the leafless trees.

"What are you thinking?" Ila said.

Hank twisted the radio dial slowly in his fingers, trying to find something to listen to. Mostly it was farm reports and grain markets, spliced with country music.

"She's the first one," Ila said. "There's lots of kids our age who've lost every single parent already."

She hadn't slept a wink in the four hours they were on the road, even if they hadn't talked that much.

"I suppose it had to happen sometime. One of them had to be first—"

Hank nodded. "Maybe that's the way I see it right now," he told her. "I feel almost ugly about it." He reached up with both hands and took the wheel right at the top. "When I thought he was dead in the woods—it was as if everything had ended or something. Now it's a fact that she's gone and all I can do is think of the business of it. You know what I mean?"

"I've always loved your mother," Ila said. "You know that. Right from the very first time we met in that restaurant at school. Right from the very beginning—"

"Who couldn't love my mother for what she had to put up with." He laughed. "She was almost angelic. Even when I was a kid I knew that. You know those things somehow. You hear other people talking about your own folks, you know?—and the way they talk, you just know what other people think. Poor woman didn't have a chance to be anything but angelic having to live with him—

"Look at that," he said, pointing at a barge slowly moving down the river through the red buoys marking the main channel.

"This isn't the time to start claiming old debts, Hank," she said. "We may have to wait seven years." She twisted herself in the seat to bring her feet up beneath her and face him. "Almost sounds biblical, doesn't it?"

"I'm going to play it by ear," he said.

The interstate swept left over the river on a massive bridge that brought them over the main channel and a half-mile or more of lakes and inlets west into Wisconsin. Even though the trees had already shed their leaves, Hank felt good again being back in the forests, as if it were easier to hide in the patchwork woods, away from the perfectly open plains.

"Are you hungry?" Ila said.

"I suppose I am."

"I could use some coffee," she told him.

They pulled into a truck stop, and Hank filled the tank while Ila ran in for a couple rolls and coffee to go. When she got back in the car, she offered to drive, but Hank said no. He figured driving gave him something simple to think about.

"You remembering what that old man said last night yet?" she said.

"I wish I could control what I'm thinking," he told her. "I wish I had this ledger to write down, in order, all the things I can afford myself time to think about. Put them all down in a list and just start at the top."

The hot coffee had a lot of bite.

"Does it bother you?" she said.

"Of course it bothers me. But it's like I don't have time for that right now." He turned to her. "You're the one that said that this won't be the time for old debts—"

"Can you help yourself?"

"I don't know. Maybe I got too much of the old man in me too."

"You better try," she said.

"I'm not sure I like being the goods in some foxhole bargain my father made with God Almighty," he told her. "Can you blame me?"

"I'm not saying that," she said.

" 'Give us another child, Lord, and we'll give him to

You.' It makes for great Bible stories, doesn't it? Samuel's poor mother never had a son, and then she gets this little one and just brings him away to the temple. Part of the bargain—something you order out of a catalogue. I bet nobody ever asked Samuel if he wanted to drive a truck. They just hauled him off to the temple, part of the bargain."

Ila brushed the crumbs from her roll off onto the floor. "He's not going to be the same man without her, Hank. You just try to remember that."

"I wish I could keep reminding myself that she's actually gone—"

"I'm going to help you," she told him. "You hear me?"

It made him break into a smile. "I'm in trouble now," he said.

"I'm serious," she said. "This isn't the time for you two to square off. Wait seven years. Somehow, I like the sound of that."

He tried to concentrate hard on what needed to be done once they would get back to Easton.

No one met them at the front porch when they pulled up, so Hank took the luggage and followed Ila through the front door without knocking. The kitchen was straight, perfectly clean, the dishrag folded twice over the basket where Corrie always stacked her plates, squeaky wet, when they came from the sink. Just one coffee cup next to the white vacuum bottle where it always stood on the counter.

His mother was gone and he knew it. The trip had taken just more than ten hours. Ila had driven the last few hours, while he slumped into the back seat, his mind dipping in and out of consciousness, as if he were stumbling through two half-obscured worlds.

When he came in through the family room and saw his mother's Wurlitzer standing there against the wall, he knew she was gone. She wasn't there at the door to meet them. No one was at the door. It was just after lunch and Corrie would have had something waiting on the stove; she would have known they would come early, even though Wim said they would be smart to wait until morning.

His mother, in her own quiet way, would have known, and right now she'd be throwing a hot dish on the range, warming it up for them. "Ja, you must be so hungry," she would have said, "ten hours of travel." Wim and Corrie had never travelled much in this country, and ten hours of travel in one day was almost inconceivable to them. "Here I have some hotdish. It will take maybe a minute or so to heat up."

But his mother was gone.

"Anybody home?" Ila said. She looked up at him when she said it, as if the volume were improper now in the house. She shrugged her shoulders. "Dad?" she said.

No one answered.

Hank set down the suitcases in the kitchen next to the hallway upstairs. He reached for an orange tumbler on the sink and turned on the water. Cold gloved his hand as water ran down over his wrist. "I'm tired," he said. "Maybe I'll just take a rest, as long as they aren't home."

"They're downstairs, Hank. Listen." Ila stood at the basement steps and held the door open. Tony's voice rose in fragments from below. Wim was working. He was working downstairs with the boy.

Hank filled the glass. In his parents' home tap water always came out clouded.

Ila cleared her breath. "Well?" she said. "You ready?"

He drank a half glass and laid the orange tumbler down on its side on the rubber mat in the sink. He listened to Tony's voice through the open basement door. "He's quite a talker, that kid," Hank said.

"You think maybe I should take him up here and let you two alone?" she said. She turned the knob back and forth in her hand slowly, as if she were trying to work it free. "Would you rather, I mean?"

"Let's go," he said, "you and me."

She held the door for him.

"Dad," he said, "Dad, we're home."

The stairway wound around the clothes chute, past coats and sweaters hanging there, lined up ready for winter, one after another, like motionless sails.

"Ja, Hank, is that you already?" Wim was sitting on his stool, his denim apron pulled around him, tied at the waist, and Tony sat next to him, eyes round as checkers, watching his grandfather shave long yellow strips from a thin column of wood with a thin blade. Wim pulled his glasses up on his forehead and squinted. "What is it that already this early you come home?" he said. "Tony and me, we didn't think you would make it till supper maybe."

"We couldn't sleep anyway. We thought we might as well start out—I mean, since we couldn't sleep anyway. It was ridiculous to stay—"

"Ridiculous! I'll tell you what is ridiculous—now look what we've got here: tomorrow the wake and then the funeral and so much yet and you both don't have much sleep to speak of. Ach, Hank, but that was stupid not to listen to me." He looked away for a minute, skinned one strip from the wood. "I thought maybe you had more sense than him, Ila."

Tony seemed not to notice them at all. His hands were on his knees, fingers spread, waiting for his grandpa to keep whittling away at what appeared to be another bird.

"Tony, your mommy's home," Ila said. "And your daddy, too."

"The both of you he forgot about already," Wim said, "because he found his grandpa. Grandma he loved, too."

"Grandma," Tony said.

"You should have seen once how it was with them.

She would read to him, every night while you were gone, and I would bring him up, you know, to bed. Except last night. It was as if she knew already before." He leaned over and put his hand on the boy's head. "But every night, Hank, every night Corrie would go up to the boy's room after the weather. Always she had to check the boy. Maybe she thought someone would steal him away from her, right out of this house." Wim chuckled to himself. "I think maybe it was that she couldn't believe in any child so beautiful. Tuesday night she says to me, 'Wim, you have to come up here once and look at him. Come now once,' she says, and she takes me by the hand—by the hand she takes me upstairs. And there he is, the boy, lying up in the crib, and his head is tucked up into the corner, all stuffed in the corner. And one of his feet is out of the crib, you know, between the bars, and around him—around his face—is this blanket. 'Look once,' Corrie says. 'Look at your grandson.'" Wim took his hand from the boy's head. "For Corrie it was like Eli with the baby Jesus and I'm not making fun. I think maybe she let herself die now that she saw him."

What surprised Hank was the way he was able to say it, as if he had known all along that she would go.

"She wasn't well. We didn't talk about it. There was always things we didn't talk about, but I knew she wasn't well. But every night she would read to him those books she bought at auction. You should have seen it."

Tony watched his grandfather scatter shavings, still oblivious to his parents' presence. He snapped the thin shavings between his fingers and dropped them individually in the old cherry can Wim used as a trashbasket.

"Tony, Mommy missed you, honey." Ila hunched down beside him and pulled him close to her. The boy pushed a handful of wood shavings in her face. "What's that?" she said. "What's Grandpa doing?"

Wim kept on carving, the shavings piling up slowly between his feet. "He wants to have the knife too sometimes," he said, "but I tell him he has to be older before Grandpa will let him carve."

When Tony smiled, Ila hugged and kissed him. He kept watching the shavings, enjoying his mother's attention.

"Tony—Grandpa's helper," Wim said. "He puts this stuff in the pail. He thinks that's pretty good that he can help Grandpa."

Sunlight came through the basement windows and brightened a square segment of the cement floor. It seemed lighter than usual downstairs. The fluorescent light was on over the workbench and the light at the base of the stairs glowed. Hank's father seemed remarkably calm, here, sitting in his world, with his grandson with him.

"What are you carving, Dad?" Hank said.

"It's a bird again, like the others. With the beak pointing straight up like this—" He raised his head and looked up at the ceiling. "When once you get a pattern done a couple of times, then the work goes so easy. A bird like this isn't so hard for me anymore. This afternoon yet I'll have this one done. But you know, Hank, once you do it so often," he stopped, pointed the knife, "once you do it so often then you don't hardly dare to try something else again. That's how it always is." He remembered his glasses up on his forehead and dropped them back over his nose. "We get used to something and just getting used to it makes us cowards. We don't want to try something new."

"Tony, Mommy brought you a present, honey. Let's go upstairs and find a new toy." Ila took Tony's hand and then turned to Wim. "I'm really sorry, Dad. I'll miss her terribly. I really loved Mom—she was so easy to love—"

Wim nodded his head in long jerks, as if everything she said was just exactly as it should have been. Ila kissed him on the forehead and took Tony away, up the stairs.

"You know, Hank, how it was—your mother always did that with you too, always checked up on you before she went to sleep, like she did with Tony." The blade crossed the grain like a glint of silver fin in the lake water, and strips of wood, tightly curled, bounced onto the cement. "That last night, she came down and she was happy." He stopped. "She didn't think it was coming, I suppose. I am sure she couldn't have known. But I think that just seeing the boy and holding him some— that was enough."

His father didn't look at him when he spoke. The blade spun off pipe-curl shavings, but Wim never looked up. Hank took a step back and sat in an old rocker, waiting.

Wim stopped carving and pulled the cherry can between his feet to catch the wood. "I remember once we had a preacher and that preacher said that we raise children to raise children—you get what that means? That was what Corrie and me did with you."

The blade slowly defined the long, thin neck.

"So what you think, Hank? Maybe now I can sit down here in my own basement and work all day long, and never again will I have to hear her: 'Wim! Wim!— this toilet doesn't work again.'" He held the wood up toward the light over the workbench, ran the blade over the curve on the bird's back. "Now all the time I get to work by myself down here. All the time. Never again an interruption. When you and Ila go again back to the field, I will be alone in my own house. Maybe I will make my own gas engine down here in my shop. You think maybe I could do that, Hank? A gas engine?" When he coughed, he held his hand up to his mouth, the blade pointed up and away from his face. "Down here I got the tools, you know. Maybe I could do it."

The figure in the wood came clearer with each stroke. Hank was amazed at how quickly his father could work.

"It's too bad you never took much to working with wood, with your hands. Here, when you grew up we had down in this basement so many tools for you to use, and lots of boys, they would have liked to use them—"

Wim didn't look any different without her, Hank thought. He sat at the edge of his stool, both legs pointed in front of him, wood shavings dropping in perfect cadence into the gold cherry can. His round face hadn't changed, nor his bald head, still slightly pointed, his thin hair pressed down flat at the sides of his head, like the last sweeps of dirty snow on a hill away from the sun. Nothing seemed to have changed on him. Hank wouldn't have been surprised to hear his mother's voice from up the stairs.

"Dad," he said, "it's really hard for me to believe that Mom is dead—"

Wim spun the knife in his hand, then drew the blade's edge across the back of his wrist. "You think maybe I don't know it, Hank? Maybe you are worried about me? So what do you think I should do? Is it crying for her?" He snapped the blade shut against his hand. "I don't cry for her, because she is gone so easily that I pray to God it will be that easy for me, too. Now she is in glory. And so easy—not even a noise, Hank. Just like this—her head fell, as if she was asleep. That's it." He rubbed his chin with the back of his wrist. "So maybe for her you want me to cry, but I won't cry for her. One minute with Tony, the next with the Lord. Just like that—bang!" He saw he had closed the knife. With his teeth he jerked the blade partly out again, then flicked it out completely with his fingers.

The fluorescent glare streaked shadows across his face. The high basement windows spread light out behind him, away from the bench.

"Corrie is with the Lord today," he said. "For no reason at all should I cry for her." The blade swept back over the long curve in the bird's neck.

"So what kind of bird is it?" he said.

Only days ago, simply the vision of a fatherless world had chilled him, pushed him stumbling through the woods like some deserted kid left bawling at the curb. His own imagination had clothed his fear in a bloody image, but now the reality of his mother's death only numbed him, blocked the reach of his grief, kept it from rising to the level he thought it should reach. He should be grief-stricken. Maybe his mother hadn't meant so much to him after all. Death was real this time, and here they sat—father and son—in this basement world, talking about a wooden bird. He wished he had learned to carve, like his father, to strip wood in sharp, clean curls.

"A loon maybe, I don't know. Long neck, long legs. It stares up to heaven. Corrie liked these birds. Sometimes she would varnish them for me down here." He pressed the wood against his knee for a minute. "You didn't know, I suppose, that Corrie helped some down here." He cleaned the blade, back and forth across his apron. "She came down here sometimes. In these last years she worked down here with me, the old machinist, with her husband. See here, Hank?" He pointed at the ceiling. "That was Corrie's light over there. For her I put it in, so we could work together." He sat back, adjusting himself on the stool.

Hank could not verify his mother's absence, because nothing in the familiar world seemed out of place. His father sat here carving a bird out of soft yellow pine. And it was quiet in the house. If he had one of Wim's dowels he could rap the low ceiling, and his mother, up in the kitchen, would jump. She was up there, he sensed. Maybe she was reading. It was impossible to think of her as being gone, because her absence had no dimensions—it was so much greater than an empty shelf or a drawer, some vacant compartment. It was too much the same in the house. He wanted the walls to weep.

"I guess I'm just happy that you're taking it so well. I just wouldn't have expected that—"

"You think maybe that I would fall apart, don't you? Corrie isn't even dead yet a day. Tomorrow she will be decked out nice in a coffin. Then she is gone in the

ground. My own son, the missionary. You have been to
the seminary—you think that your father doesn't believe
the promise of the resurrection?" He faced Hank, his
eyes less stern than inquisitive. "You think maybe death
is something to fear? Ach, Hank, though. You are the
preacher."

"The funeral is on Saturday?"

"Norman Jenke, he says, maybe it can be either Saturday or Monday. 'What do you think, Wim?' he says. So I
tell him on Saturday. She is gone now anyway. Life is to
be lived. So it is on Saturday." With the back of his hand,
he butted his glasses up off the end of his nose. Maybe if
you got to be somewhere on Sunday, Hank, you can call
it off. I think—I think I would like maybe to have you
home this Sunday. Church on Sunday alone—I don't like
to think of that." He brought the shaped wood up closer
to his eyes and trimmed at the back—short, quick
strokes, squinting.

"And Christmas, Hank. Ila's folks, they will understand if you come here Christmas. I am alone now, you
know. I think they will understand if I tell you to come
here for Christmas."

His voice was strung with the same authority, the
same immigrant persistence. Even that hadn't changed
with Corrie gone, not really. Maybe it was that Hank
expected some softening, maybe just hesitation, a dimin-
ished sense of will. But it was all there yet, here in his
basement, that old bullying diction anyway—"They will
understand if I *tell* you to come here—"

Hank waited, rocking, watching the bird being drawn
from the wood.

"So tell me, Hank, how was it out in those churches?
Good crowds I bet out there on the road?" Wim didn't
look up at him. It wasn't like him not to speak with his
eyes.

"Not so great then, maybe. Well, you know it is not
so easy always to get people out to church for week-
nights. That silly television is there in the middle of life.

You would be shocked, I think, to know who is there on the living room floor with his nose in that box all night. Even the good ones—"

Hank simply couldn't keep it inside. "I met a man you grew up with. In Ashland. In Minnesota. Lubbers—Anton Lubbers."

Wim nodded as if the man stood here between them. "Anton Lubbers. Sure, Anton Lubbers. Years ago already his wife—she wanted to move back to Minnesota so bad. Nobody can live with a wife in a long face. It can't be done."

Discretion he had always held in spades, Hank thought. He had always been reluctant to hurt his own father—the commandments there echoing in him from thousands of childhood sermons: "Honor thy father and mother and thy days shall be long . . ." Yet, Wim was different now, alone without his wife. His eyes spent all their attention on the carving. He was a different man, even if he didn't understand the changes himself, even if he tried, believer that he was, to hide behind the theology of the resurrection. The longer Hank watched him carve the bird—mechanically, as if his machinist's hands needed to be employed—the clearer he understood that the growl in the old man's admonitions was hollow, and vulnerable; it curled up at his feet. Corrie was gone. But Wim had refused to let him feel her absence, so his was the same voice that filled every chapter of Hank's own life. This time, thought Hank, he wasn't going to let it roll along merrily again. He wouldn't accept that steely way the old man had forged to be the father of a chosen son.

"Why didn't you ever tell me I had a sister?" he said.

Wim turned the knife in his hand and clicked his thumb across the blade, testing its sharpness.

"Lubbers tell you that, I suppose—" Both hands dropped to his thighs. "Years ago I thought to tell you, and one day I said to Corrie that you should know or sure enough sometime you would yourself find out." His face turned balky and blank. "But maybe it was that I just forgot to tell you." He sat up straight and tucked his feet beneath the stool. "It must be hard for you to believe that—I mean that maybe we just forgot to tell you something so important, but some things don't come up so easy, even if they are never really behind you."

"I don't understand it," Hank said. "I mean, I'm grown up now. I've been a man for years—"

He stood the bird on the bench and picked the whetstone from a shelf, rubbing it slowly between his thumb and fingers. "Corrie would never speak of the baby. I mean, inside of me I knew long ago that it would be wrong to speak of it to her again—it would be wrong even to bring it up. Some things stand up in front of you like brick walls, and they stay there, and sometimes you just try to live like it's just a box, maybe, with that one wall there. You don't try to break it down. You live with it. Like the lake, you know. It's always out there east of us. So we got no east here on the lakeshore, only the lake. That's how it is with—"

"I deserved to know sometime—"

"We never told you—maybe we never told you because we forgot such things should be talked about." Wim never looked up at all but watched the stone in his fingers. "I think that's why, Hank. We forgot that we could say those things, that it happened in this world here, in Easton." He spit on the stone and rubbed the blade three, four times across the spot.

"I'm sorry I had to find out that way," Hank said. "I'm sorry it had to be right now, I mean with all the rest of the pain—"

"What do you know about pain, Hank? You're just a boy yet. You don't know pain. Nothing. None of you, you young ones. You can't even speak of pain. For close to fifty years, it's like that first baby never lived at all in her. Yet, her crying is here yet in my ears. And my father's crying. He never knew English at all. *'In verwachting,'* he said to me, and that look, you know, on his face, as if your mother and I had turned our souls over to Satan.

"He cried too—with my mother. We told them. We had to." He put everything down on the bench and sat with his hands empty, staring up at Hank. "You listen—there they sat in the kitchen, both of them crying because it was such a big thing then, a pregnant girl with their son—Corrie *in verwachting*. I was eighteen maybe. Working—hired man. And Corrie's mother and father too, they had to be told. And the church in those days.

"And then the baby dies. Too young, huh? Too young to live yet in this world of sin. And then more crying, of course. For fifty years, Hank—Corrie and I, we never talked of it—only, when I said to her once that you should know."

"What did she say?"

"Nothing. She didn't talk one word. That was her answer. No answer, just that look on her face, gray like an old pail. To Corrie, it was retribution that the child should die." He pulled his hands together on his lap and rubbed his fingers as if they were cold. "Today you laugh at such foolishness, but it was something she never could forget—not that baby dying so little." He put up his hands to judge the size.

"Maybe I should be sorry because some man in Minnesota tells you the story, and today already you are thirty years old. Maybe it was wrong not to tell you. I should have told you once, maybe in the woods on those long walks we would take. Away from Corrie. But lots of time in life you got these choices, Hank, and they aren't always so easy as they seem maybe today, when it all looks so terrible clear. Maybe it's a choice you got between Tony and Ila, you know. What to say—" He reached up for his glasses, slipped them off, looked at the lenses as if to count the nicks from metal splinters.

"How should I say it?—you get used to not talking and finally the whole story gets hidden in the silence." He retrieved the knife and the whetstone, still damp and dark in the middle, in the thin spot where every blade had been sharpened. "Maybe that's the way the Lord would have it, see? Maybe He didn't need me to have to tell you something like that. So now you know, and I can sleep easy too because I never hurt Corrie. I never told you—"

"I'm not angry—"

The soft swish of the knife on the stone stopped whenever Wim flipped the edge.

"Maybe nothing would have been different if I had known before. It's just that it was such a surprise—like a shock to find out something that everybody else knows about you, but you never knew yourself—"

Wim dropped the whetstone on the bench and retrieved the wood. "Close to fifty years Corrie won't talk about that baby. It is so close in her like that—" He pointed with the thick base of the bird. "Let me tell you once, what it has to do with you. Twenty years we waited for you, even me. You know how it was—I told you—how we thought it was like Abraham and Sarah. We were so old and no children. As if the Lord had said there would be no more after the tiny one that died so little. I know Corrie thought it was that way. I know she did, because she never said it."

The bird's neck seemed to lengthen slowly.

"And sometimes I would get angry with God. Like Moses—I felt like Moses. He can't go himself to the land of promise for one little error. There he stands up on the mountain, ready to die, while his people go straight into the land of milk and honey. And we sit there in church and watch all the others have children. With Corrie it was too much pain. We sat once next to the Hendricks family, when they had a little one, and halfway through, right in the middle of worship, Corrie walks out and I know why so I don't even go after her. I don't have to know from her own mouth what happens, because what it is she felt was there in my own heart— to see that little one next to her, sucking like that." He brought his thumb up to his mouth, showing a fist. "Some things you don't talk about, Hank.

"And then Corrie was what—forty-three years old? And she misses for two months. 'Corrie,' I say, 'you better see the doctor,' but she says, no, because she is always late and never right on time with her monthly, and she doesn't like him poking her, you know. But that's not all either. She can't go because it would be death to know that it wasn't a child there in her—"

He rubbed the back of his hand across his temple.

"But she is pregnant. Sure enough if she isn't once more *in verwachting*—" He laid his palms flat on his thighs as if he were suddenly surprised again. "The Lord gave us that answer to prayer right there in her. We knew it."

Wim stood from the stool and leaned against the bench, the knife in one fist and the carving in the other. "I wish that she was here now, Hank." He pulled breath from deep in his chest. "I wish she was here to hear all of this because it is something that we never talked about—even though we are alone and together for all those years."

Every line made Hank feel stronger. He felt as if he were growing right into the ceiling.

"I don't like to remember that time either, when she carried you. I would never choose to live that part of my life over either. Forever she worried then: sometimes sure that what is moving inside her is forgiveness; then sometimes she thinks she is sure she will have trouble like with the first. 'Wim,' she says late in the night, 'maybe for too long the baby hasn't moved. Wim, wake up. Wim!' " He raised both hands over his head, and he laughed to remember it—not aloud really, as if right now to laugh aloud would offend a memory.

"But there is no problems. You were a healthy boy, Hank. I can see you yet in that carton in the hospital, and when I visit Corrie on Thursday, when you were already three days old and your eyes, clear and bright, like you could see it all in front of you. Then one day I'm in the hospital and Corrie is nursing you, and your little hand, here it lies up here on her chest. And Corrie says to me, 'Wim,' she says, 'this one is a miracle. This one is a gift of grace,' she says.

" 'Corrie,' I say, 'you show me one in this hospital that is not such a gift.'

"And she looks down at you, you know, at your face, and your mouth is going, pumping at her breast. 'No, Wim,' she says, 'I mean this one is special. This one belongs to the Lord.' "

He stopped talking and put his hand up over his eyes, his face down toward the shavings. He breathed long and hard through his nose. "She's gone now," he said, holding himself stiffly. "It's a time when I have to learn to live without her."

Once more he removed his glasses, rubbing the back of his hand through his eyes. "I remember smiling with her then, right there in the hospital, because for me it is maybe the most beautiful thing in this world to see what I see, this miracle of birth, this boy here, and now he is a man, a missionary.

"Corrie sits up in bed and you are nursing and everyone is healthy and I say to her, 'This one belongs to the Lord, Corrie.' "

He looked down at his hands and seemed embarrassed to see the knife bound in his fingers.

"You were a miracle child, Hank. Corrie always said that you were special, a gift of grace." He turned the knife and took short jerks at the base of the carving, but his sweaty hands seemed dismembered from his arms, as if they belonged to someone else. He rubbed them together.

"You should have told me, Dad. You should have told me all of that long ago. It makes some sense now—"

"Always we considered you a gift of grace. 'This one

belongs to God,' Corrie used to say. Before she went to bed she would check on you every night, like she did with Tony. And some nights I would go up with her. 'This one belongs to the Lord,' she would say when you laid there in your crib."

Hank's hands and feet felt stiff, as if nuts and bolts too tightly snugged held him unable to bend. Maybe it was grace itself that stood between them all those years, God's own grace that pieced them together as caricatures in one another's eyes. His heart seemed too large, and his pulse so heavy it throbbed in his neck.

"Why didn't you let me be a kid, Dad?" he said.

Wim's face went blank again.

"All of it you did in the name of the Lord. All of it! I know you did." He felt as if the basement were some old balcony that shook with every footstep.

"It's clear now—do you see what it's done to you and me? You never thought of me as a boy, never. I was always like some tiny congregation waiting for a sermon. I mean, you wanted me to be some gift of grace, some barely physical answer to prayer. So all my life, even today, you treat me as if I am simply a soul, some odd pale physical essence, something to yell at, something to offer to God. I'm special. All my life I've been special. You gave me to God—sure you did, but you never once asked me if that's where I wanted to go. Choice was an unaffordable luxury, wasn't it? It would have been a gamble, because to lose me would be to lose your own forgiveness. You spent your whole life making me perfect, as if your preaching could sanctify me and you at the same time."

Wim eyes narrowed in a kind of intensity that Hank had never really seen before. "I took you to the woods and hunting. I was a father—"

"For object lessons. 'See that, Hank—ha! ha! You can't hit those ducks out there—let that be a lesson to you. All of us, we have perspective, you see!' Everything a lesson. Forever you were bringing me up. You never let me grow. So I am a gift of grace—maybe so, but I was a child, too." It was all there now. The whole business— the gift of grace. He had always felt the barrier between them, but he had never recognized its real character. "So when does it stop? When is it over, this obligation of yours to repay the Lord Almighty? We've been in missions for seven years, but even that's not enough. Even today you keep hammering away all the time, trying to make me perfect—"

Wim stared at him, his tongue flat in his open mouth. Tony's feet slapped over the kitchen floor above them.

"I understand now. I understand the way you're always acting toward me, all our bloody arguments, even my life I understand, because I was never a kid. I was always a gift of grace, and I'm not so sure if that's more or less than being human."

Hank leaned forward in the chair and pushed himself up with his hands. Wim looked down, his elbows on his knees, the knife and the bird still gripped in either hand.

He felt as if he were leaning into a stiff wind when he turned away from his father, a cold wind that shook him with the odd fear that behind him there was still too much to be said.

"So maybe I wasn't so good as a father, Hank, but look once what you are today. This whole town is proud of you, Hank. Everyone is proud of Hank Pietenpol, the missionary."

The stool's metal feet squealed across the cement when his father dropped back down before the bench.

"So maybe you don't like it much, the way I raised you. But now you have a boy too—you and Ila—and someday the Lord God will ask you if you did everything to bring up that boy in the fear of the Lord's name. Someday you and I will stand there together, Hank—the both of us fathers."

Two steps up he felt weightless, hanging between two

magnetic fields, upstairs the peace of escaping him and downstairs, behind him, the possibility of finally concluding a lifetime of warfare by standing here and screaming down at the man until some whit of truth made it through the perfect armor of his father's faith.

"Hank—you listen! Maybe I don't care what it is you think of me now. I don't care one bit. But Corrie said you were—"

"Don't blame your eternal sermons on my mother—"

"And you don't talk to your father that way—" Wim stabbed the knife in the workbench. "I won't have you talking to me like that in my own house." The bird shook in his fist when he walked to the stairs. "All I care is that with you I did my duty to God. It was what I was called to do—to bring you up for God. It was what I did—God helping me. I did what I was called to do and now one day when I, like Corrie, meet the Lord, on that last day, I can stand before Him when it comes to my turn, and I can say, 'Lord, forgive me, but I did everything what I could possible to bring that boy up in the fear of the Father.' "

"You used me, Dad—"

Wim's face bent up towards him defiantly. "I stand here forgiven. When I look up to God, I feel His grace. I got no need to ask forgiveness of you."

"You used me, you know that? You used me—"

He fumbled with the bird, then held the base in his right hand. "Can you do this, Hank? Can you look to heaven like this, as you stand here now with hate in your heart?" He pushed the carving into Hank's face. "I can look up, Hank. I can look to heaven because all things work together for good—"

Slowly, he withdrew it. "You do it now, for me. You look up to God and say that there is no doubt in your soul. Go on. You are the missionary—"

Hank's chest pumped as he looked into the stolid face of his father's supreme confidence.

"You take this one here, Hank. You take this one, you hear. Maybe it isn't done, but you take it, and you put it somewhere in your house, because it must remind you that nothing is so important as that someday you can look to God like this. Not beautiful either, not some pretty prayer for nice people to hear, but that you can look up to God Almighty and say that you did everything in your power for the Lord."

Wim pushed the wooden statue out before his face. "Take it," he said. "You hear me? Take it."

As commanded, he took the bird and turned it in his hands, its unfinished body rough-cast and coarse. "You used me as your atonement, Dad, don't you see? You gave me to the Lord like the ram in the thicket. You used me, a sacrifice to make your peace with God. For your silly guilt—"

"Look once at what you are, Hank. For seven years a missionary to the heathen in El Salvador. I have this to comfort me: my son has given his life to God's work. So sometimes I would push you too hard, I don't know. But look at what you are, Hank."

Hank reached for the wall. "I'm not going back, Dad," he said.

Wim's eyes glistened into defiance.

"I'm not going back. You hear me?"

He closed his lips under his nose, and his face dropped down toward his chest in an uneven series of short jerks. He turned away from the stairs and walked to the workbench, his feet edging over the cement as if he were afraid to lift them too high, away from the hard floor.

Hank turned the wood in his hand and went up past the winter coats, past Wim's plaid hunting jacket, on his way upstairs to the kitchen, to Corrie's room.

And stood there at the door and waited for things to settle inside. The cessation never brought peace. Always there was hunger, that incessant desire to be able to call it all back, all the words, and file them in some corner, as if everything he had said still hung up in the room beneath him like a row of hind quarters steadily rotting in the damp quiet of the basement. And inside there was nothing to stanch the hurt.

"Tony's sleeping," Ila said, her voice floating from the family room.

Corrie was gone, of course. His mother was dead, he had to remind himself. Somehow he had forgotten. His mother was dead, her body lying in the mortuary now—Norman Jenke standing over it the way his father stood over a dead animal, doing whatever morticians do to make a body fit for showing.

"How did it go?" Ila said it from the living room. There was some comfort in her woman's voice. She slumped over the edge of the couch, half reclining, as if she might be trying to get some sleep. "What happened?" she said.

"It's not over," he said. He sat in a chair and faced her.

"What's that thing in your hand?" she said.

He looked at it for a minute, wrapped his fingers around it. "I could break this thing, you know. In one hand, I could break it in two pieces, Ila."

"What is it?"

"It's a sermon. It's a sermon." He flexed his fist on the wood. "This is pine, Ila. I could break it, this yellow wood, in my fingers."

"Why would you want to do that?"

He held it so tightly with his fist that he could feel it bend between his fingers. "It's that easy," he said. "I could snap it just so easily." In his fist it felt like pliable steel.

"What good is there in snapping it?" Ila said.

He held it there momentarily, then loosened his grip and took it in both hands. "Stupid thing," he said. Its back was nicked and burred. It called for sanding. He sat it down on the table next to his chair.

"It doesn't stand straight. It's not even finished, is it?"

she said. "How come he gave you something that wasn't even finished?"

"Hank?" Wim's voice rang up the steps, amplified by the empty stairwell. "Hank?" They could hear his feet on the wood stairs.

Hank stretched his arms out to the side and dropped his head back on the chair.

Wim had his apron off, and his glasses in his fingers. "Hank," he said. His breath came in slow, deep drafts. "You mind if I sit here with you?" He pointed to his own chair.

"Dad—" Ila said, as if it were an insulting question.

"When my father died I was nineteen, the oldest. I remember the people brought over whole meals to my mother. For two weeks all over the kitchen, cakes and muffins and pies. The kids would bother my mother— 'Ma,' they would say, 'a little piece of cake?' After the funeral, Aaldert asked her again, and maybe that time my mother was tired from all the business. 'Aaldert,' she says, 'you eat all the cake you want today because how often does your father die anyway?' And then we laughed. It was such a bad joke for her, but we laughed. She didn't mean it that way." His glasses flashed in front of him in his hands. He waited. "Sometimes we say things that maybe we don't believe, I mean in a time like this present."

Corrie's chair was an empty space, of course, the wrinkle-less tapestry she draped it with squared perfectly.

"It's hard to feel that she's gone, Dad," Ila said. "I mean you just keep expecting her to come in here and serve coffee. I can't imagine that she's not coming back."

Wim pulled the bows of his glasses back over his ears. "I know it in the basement, because all the time down there I know when I come up she won't be here. And I know it in my bed, and I know it here in this room." His eyes followed imaginary lines around the living room, slowly, as if some living remnant of his wife might still be there to speak for her. "But it's not so bad that she's gone, Hank. That's not so bad, really—we know where she is." He rubbed his fingers into his eyes, beneath the lenses of his glasses.

"I suppose when something like this happens, a Christian man like myself cries more for himself than for anything else. I'm the one alone now—"

"It's all right, Dad. It's all right." Ila sat forward in her chair.

"I did everything best I could to raise you, and this anger in you I don't understand. Maybe sometimes too bossy I was, I don't know. But right now I am alone here in my own house for this first time in fifty years—"

Ila came to Wim and sat on her knees, her arms around him.

"So one time I will ask you, Hank. Now is a time when you can't hate me—I don't care what you think of your father. Please. Now it is that I need my only son."

They slumped together, Ila and Wim, wrapped in each other, and for the first time in his life Hank felt himself towering over his father, composed, assured that all these tight years behind him were as clear as the future he had once never doubted. He was the stronger now, because he had control. It lay in his own power to hold his father like a loved one. It was at last his own choice. He could break the man now—railing for railing.

There was a shot in the woods, and an old man in a plaid jacket lay face down in the snow.

"It doesn't matter anyway, Hank, what you think of me, because you have to forgive, you know. I brought you up to know, and whatever it is that makes you angry with me, you have to forgive. Like it or not, you know that. I got comfort because I know you."

And just like that, whatever penitence or contrition may have been there on Wim's face was washed away in the flood of assurance the old man had in his God *and* his only child, the boy he had shaped and bent to fit a mold he would be forever confident God himself had set, a confidence that showed in a wiry smile, stoic but sincere, accommodating and determined. A forgiven smile.

"It's hard for me, you know, to say those things to you. I'm an old Calvinist who's not so good at confession." Wim smiled at Ila, and she took her arms away slowly.

"This being alone I got to get used to now, and pretty soon cooking my own dinner." He sat up at the edge of the chair. "Maybe I take the gun case back up here now, Hank. What do you think—"

Ila smiled. "It doesn't match the furniture anymore, Dad," she said.

And when he rose from the chair, he stood straight and thick as an old jetty piling still upright in the constant wash of lake waves.

"I have to finish that bird, Hank," he said. "What good is it to have something like that in the house—it doesn't even look yet like anything." He picked up the carving and ran his fingers over the neck. "No legs here yet," he said.

"Just let it, Dad. Start on something else. All the time you'll have now, who knows?—maybe you'll start another business yet." Hank held out his hand for the carving. "Make a gas engine down there."

"You let me find one for you that is done then. Ila doesn't want this—half-carved and scratchy."

"That one is finished," Hank said. "That's the one I want. You put a date on the bottom, but don't touch it with a knife."

Wim looked at Ila as if the man she had married was strange.

When Wim went back downstairs, Ila put on the coffee. Hank thought it would be good for the three of them to sit at Corrie's kitchen table together.